PROMISE PENDING

PROMISE PENDING

•

Gail MacMillan

AVALON BOOKS
THOMAS BOUREGY AND COMPANY, INC.
401 LAFAYETTE STREET
NEW YORK, NEW YORK 10003

PRINTED IN THE UNITED STATES OF AMERICA
ON ACID-FREE PAPER
BY HADDON CRAFTSMEN, BLOOMSBURG, PENNSYLVANIA

To my friend, colleague, and husband, Ron, and our three
wonderful children, Joan, Carol, and Steve.

Chapter One

"Could you marry this man?" Editor Teddi Walsh held up the eight-by-ten-inch black-and-white glossy and looked sharply at the slender young woman standing on the other side of the big mahogany desk.

"Ummm..." Leaning forward to more closely peruse the photo of the tall, muscular man leaning, arms akimbo, against a white birch on the edge of what appeared to be a wilderness lake, Vanessa narrowed intense green eyes and pursed soft pink lips. "Actually he looks too

3

good to be true, the type that can fall in love only with their own image in a mirror. But why are you asking me? Susan Jennings does the 'Could You Marry This Man' feature.''

''Unfortunately, on her last assignment, Susan found a man she could indeed marry.'' Teddi sent the photo flying across the desk toward the younger woman and sighed. ''I was afraid that Texas billionaire might be too hard for her to resist. Now I'm left with no one to take over our most popular item. So how about it? Think you can?''

Completely astonished, Vanessa picked up the picture and gave it a more serious scrutiny. The man was about thirty, she guessed, nicely filling out jeans and a plaid shirt in all the right places. His light brown hair was sun-streaked, either from exposure to the elements or a beautician's chemicals. And handsome, too ruggedly handsome to be for real. He could have played the lead in any one of the romantic

4

films she had seen lately. A self-absorbed Narcissus who never dirtied his manicure or let the wind ruffle his hair, she thought contemptuously as she returned her attention to the woman behind the desk.

Teddi Walsh herself was a handsome creature. She could have been an anchorwoman for any of the major television networks here in New York, Vanessa decided. Blond, slender, faultlessly groomed, and coolly sophisticated, the forty-five-year-old had as much professional polish as any of the stories she submitted for her publisher's approval. She looked as if she definitely belonged in the elegant office that was her home with Wainwright Publishing.

"You're asking me to take over a top-of-the-line job just like that?" Vanessa asked, not quite able to believe what was being offered to her and by whom.

"Why not?" Teddi affected an off-handedness Vanessa knew she didn't feel. Giving out an assignment of this importance was far from a casual matter. Teddi's position as editor of *Today's Trends*, a women's magazine with a circulation of over two hundred thousand, rested on each and every writer and story she represented to James Wainwright, her hard-driving publisher. It was a job Teddi loved and had worked long and hard to get, Vanessa knew only too well.

"Because this will be my first major piece," she replied. "All I've done since I finished journalism school and came to New York to work is edit copy in your advertising department. At college I wasn't exactly cited for my talent, either. Susan Jennings was a seasoned pro. I'm hardly an obvious choice to follow in her footsteps."

"Are you implying I'm playing favorites?" Teddi Walsh's green eyes narrowed dangerously as she arose to face the young woman.

"No, Mom . . . that is . . ." Vanessa was suddenly stammering, thrown off balance as she always was when her mother reverted from caring mother to pure professional.

"Well, so what if I am?" The editor came around the massive desk to stand in front of her daughter. "Don't you think I've earned the right to take a calculated risk on an aspiring new writer? And, Vannie, please don't call me Mom again in this building or we could both be unemployed. Mr. Wainwright was adamant about our keeping a professional profile while we're on the premises."

"If I don't pull this off, you'll be in a lot deeper trouble than for just allowing yourself to be called Mom on the job," Vanessa said, understanding the extent of her mother's commitment. "You stuck your neck far enough into the noose when you hired me. This could be the jolt that knocks the stool from under your feet. You worked so hard to get this job; I don't want to jeopardize it in any way."

Teddi shrugged. "What's life without

a few risks? Anyway, I know you'll be great. You come from terrific stock.''

''Then if you're certain, rest assured I'll do my best,'' Vanessa replied with commitment. ''I won't let you down, I promise.''

''Now don't get melodramatic.'' Teddi turned quickly away, and Vanessa suppressed a grin. For all her sophistication, good old Mom had never been great at handling emotional moments. ''And, Vannie, you're not on Grandma's farm in Maine now.'' She glanced back significantly at her jeans-clad daughter with a thick braid of light brown hair curling over the shoulder of her faded blue plaid shirt. ''You're a representative of this magazine. It's time you looked the part. I've made an appointment for you with my beautician. You're due there in an hour. After that, take my charge card and outfit yourself properly.''

''It doesn't look as if I'll need any fancy clothes on this assignment,''

8

Vanessa replied as she turned the picture over in her hands and began to read the write-up on the back. "It says this guy, Barret Madison, is a research biologist in a wilderness park in New Brunswick, Canada, and that he lives in an isolated log cabin on the edge of the lake in the photo."

She turned the picture back over and looked closely at the background of lake and mountains. Then her gaze traveled to the man and suddenly she discovered something she hadn't noticed before.

It was his eyes, eyes that sparkled with something she couldn't quite categorize as wit or wickedness or a mixture of both. They told her he was definitely no mere pretty face, no one-dimensional Marlboro Man. And suddenly he intrigued her.

"I take it you've checked him out and you've found he's no ax murderer or social outcast." She tried to hide her rising interest with lightly sarcastic banter.

"Of course." Teddi stood gazing out

9

her twelfth-floor window and brushed an imaginary speck of dust from the lapel of her immaculate red suit jacket. ''Do you think I'd send you into the wilderness with a man who had anything less than a squeaky-clean reputation?''

''But why this guy?'' Vanessa asked. ''According to his write-up, he's no celebrity. The 'Could You Marry' section has always featured viable marriage prospects for successful career women. In the last two years, Susan Jennings has always chosen to profile millionaires, media stars, and sports personalities. From the write-up, this guy is none of the above.''

''No, but he's a dedicated environmentalist,'' Teddi replied, turning back to face her daughter. ''With all the emphasis these days on the destruction of the rain forest, his work is of interest to anyone concerned about the future of our planet, as, hopefully, all our readers are. He's currently fighting big government and big industry to save a wilderness area. That makes him a hero, a rebel with a very just cause.''

''I agree, but will your readers, today's upwardly mobile career types, see him that way?''

''I'm gambling that they will,'' she said frankly. ''I admit, however, I am going out a long way on the proverbial limb by selecting Barret Madison as December's Mr. Could You Marry guy. And when Susan did a disappearing act on me, I had to look around for someone who could work with this man, appreciate his lifestyle, and come up with an appealing piece. Almost immediately I thought of you.''

''Why?'' Vanessa met her mother's green eyes squarely. ''The truth, Mrs. Walsh, if you please.''

''Certainly.'' Teddi perched on the corner of her desk, one shapely leg swinging nonchalantly. ''You're the outdoorsy type. You flourished when you lived with Mom and Dad on their farm. And your

11

grandparents developed such an appreci-
ation of nature in you, for a while I feared
the world of journalism might lose you to
some environmentalist pursuit.''

''And I was the only writer in this entire, vast publishing house with those
qualifications?'' Vanessa refused to remove her penetrating gaze from her
mother.

''Well, no, but—''

''Come clean, Mom. You thought I
needed to get away for a while, didn't
you?''

''Vannie . . .''

''Mom, I can talk about it now.'' Vanessa gave her braid an aggressive fling
over her shoulder. ''Wade Johnson is old
news . . . bad, old news.''

''Vanessa, I know how hurt you were,
but believe me, not all men are like him.
You can't let bitterness ruin your chances
of sharing your life with someone worth-
while and interesting and exciting.''

"Like Colin Walsh." Vanessa's tone softened as she spoke her father's name.

"Like Colin Walsh," Teddie agreed, and Vanessa saw the instant softening in her mother's expression that always occurred when she spoke of her handsome, international journalist husband.

"Where is Dad at present?" Vanessa asked in an attempt to divert the conversation from Wade Johnson.

"Somewhere in the Middle East." Teddi tried to feign nonchalance but failed. "He's due home in a few weeks. We're going to convince him to stay for Christmas."

"Definitely . . . up at Pop and Gram's farm as usual, I hope." Vanessa was always eager to return to her grandparents' farm, where she had grown up while her parents pursued their careers in New York and abroad.

"Definitely. What would Christmas be without Maine and snow and your grandpa's horses pulling a sleigh? But now you'd better go. You have a lot to do between now and noon tomorrow.''

''Noon tomorrow?'' Astonished, Vanessa sank into a chair near the door. ''You don't mean I'm leaving so soon?''

''Of course.'' Teddi slid off the desk and stood up, straight and commanding. ''This is the media ... stories must be immediate.''

''Mom, are you sure you're not rushing me off just because Wade is back in New York?'' she asked. ''I did watch the news last night. I saw him in that writhing mass of photojournalists chasing the Duchess of York around the airport. Do you really think I'd be dumb enough to get involved with him again?'' But try as she might, Vanessa could not prevent her voice from rising sharply toward the end of the question.

''Honey, you thought you were in love with him; you were talking marriage. When a woman allows herself to get that serious about a man, she doesn't forget him overnight, no matter—"

"No matter what a jerk he turns out to be?" Vanessa broke in. "No matter that he was only romancing me in the hopes of getting a job on my father's famous team of journalists, no matter that his genuine significant other was your former secretary, who knew Dad's schedules and tastes almost as well as we do. Oh, he was smooth, I'll give him that . . . until that night I decided to surprise him in his apartment with a birthday cake. . . ."

Vanessa stopped abruptly as the scalding pain came flooding back. In her mind she was again in the kitchen of Wade's apartment, a birthday cake and champagne in the fridge, a small book of romantic poems wrapped in green paper in her hands.

Again she heard the door open and felt her heart shrivel as a woman's laughter pealed into the living room, recognized Jennifer Leslie's voice . . . Jennifer, her mother's secretary, who had introduced her to Wade when she had first come to New York . . . heard Wade's suggestive, bantering remarks, and then his soul-rending jest about "romancing the old man's little country bumpkin" until he got a job on Colin Walsh's crack news team, then how it would be just him and Jenny all the way.

"Vanessa, he isn't worth a second's consideration." Teddi was instantly by her daughter's side. "Actually some good came out of the matter. I discovered Jennifer Leslie wasn't to be trusted, that she was going through my personal notes for information on Colin. No one needs that kind of secretarial assistance."

"Thanks, Mom." Vanessa cleared her throat and arose. "Now, moving right along, I guess I'd better get to that beauty salon—a new look to go along with my new outlook."

"New outlook?" Teddi raised deli-

16

cately arched eyebrows in concern. ''What do you mean?''

''You've just offered me an excellent opportunity to change my style once and for all,'' Vanessa said brightly, too brightly. ''No more innocent little country girl from Maine, ready to swoon over the first handsome, worldly man she meets. No sirree, ma'am. From now on, I'm Vanessa Walsh, professional journalist, New York cool and sophisticated.''

She picked up her shabby backpack, slung its strap over her shoulder, and headed for the door.

''Don't worry, Mrs. Walsh,'' she said, her voice hard, cold, and confident. ''I promise I won't do a Susan Jennings on you, especially with a guy who looks like that!'' She made a contemptuous gesture at the photo lying on the desk. ''In fact I'll write you a story as clinical and detached as my last, prize-winning biology term paper in high school.''

Then she swept out of the room.

''Vannie—'' Her mother began to protest, but her words were snapped off by the sharp click of the door.

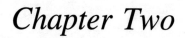

Chapter Two

The door of the small airport waiting room opened abruptly, letting in a gust of whirling fog. A tall, broad-shouldered figure appeared in silhouette against the gossamer cloud. Startled, Vanessa felt her breath catch in her throat.

"Miss Walsh?" The outline spoke, materialized into a man, and stepped confidently into the cold little room. Instantly shock and dismay flooded over the young woman shivering on the plastic chair by the window.

Good Lord, this can't be Barret Mad-

ison, she thought. This couldn't possibly be the suave, perfectly groomed creature in the photo Teddi had shown her. From the battered Snowy River hat pulled low on his forehead to the dirty sage green field coat, mud-spattered bush pants, and steel-toed work boots, the man looking inquiringly at her might easily have just stepped out of a scene in *Deliverance.*

"Mr. Madison?" She tried to clear her choked throat with the words. This had to be a messenger, she told herself, someone sent to pick her up.

"Right."

With a single word he destroyed her desperate hope. And when he strode across the room to stand a couple of feet in front of her, he did nothing to relieve the horrible first impression he had made. He sported a stubble of scraggly beard and looked so rumpled and unkempt she found herself wondering when he had last showered or indulged in any acts of hygiene. *How could Teddi have glitched so badly in checking this guy out?* she wondered, appalled.

"Sorry I'm late," he said, extending a weathered hand. "I was unexpectedly delayed."

"I understand," she heard herself replying with a confidence she was far from feeling. "It's an unpleasant night." She accepted his hand and felt its warmth encompass her cold fingers. His grasp was firm and confident, definitely not the handshake of a man who had any self-doubts. Vanessa felt a tremor that was half apprehension, half excitement course through her.

Startled at her reaction, she looked up quickly and found herself confronted with eyes as gray as the fog swirling about the small airline terminal—startlingly clear, penetrating eyes that seemed astray in the bearded, weathered face.

Then she became aware that he was returning her inspection. His expression, however, registered none of the surprise she felt certain hers did. Rather the stern set of his lips and a slight nod to himself seemed to indicate he was satisfied, had been vindicated in his expectations about her appearance.

"Nice suit," he said as she came to her senses and withdrew her hand from his. "Not really backcountry wear, but still very nice . . . for New York."

She caught a hint of something in his eyes and tone that she couldn't quite pin down as sarcasm, humor, or a mix of both.

"I have other clothes in my bags," she said defensively, feeling suddenly over-dressed in her tan pantsuit and rust-colored turtleneck. She did, however, feel confident that her new hairstyle—short, layered, and subtly highlighted—gave her a mature, professional appearance the long braid had failed to accomplish. Teddi had been right on that score, at least.

"I hope so," he replied, and this time there was definitely a note of amused satisfaction in his voice. "Otherwise I'll be forced to lend you some of mine, and the fit might be just a shade off."

She felt herself growing warm under his annoying remarks and had to remind herself sharply of her promise to her mother. She was granted a reprieve from his observations by the terminal manager.

"Hey, Barry, how's the road up to the park?" the ticket agent called out from across the room. Eager to be rid of his lingering guest, he had begun closing up shop the minute Barret Madison had arrived. The only other passenger on the twelve-seater commuter flight that had brought Vanessa to the one-room terminal had departed immediately upon arrival, a happy young wife and two children who had been eagerly awaiting his arrival in tow.

"Not bad, Jim," he replied, turning from Vanessa to face the man. "A few potholes, nothing out of the ordinary. You should bring Ellen and the kids up more

25

often. It's beautiful with the leaves changing color. They're at their best for only a few days, you know. First heavy wind or rain and they'll be gone.''

''I know, I know. Just as soon as I can get someone to watch this place for a few hours, we'll be up. By the way, I heard those poachers got another bunch of trees last night. If this keeps up, there'll be no leaves left to see.''

''They are causing a lot of damage to a rare and valuable species,'' Barret agreed, and tiredly removed his dirty, wet hat to run an agitated hand through thick brown hair. ''Not to mention the sugar maples they're slicing up needlessly in search of the bird's-eye type.''

''Someone is poaching bird's-eye maples?'' Vanessa asked, instantly interested. ''That's the type of wood they use to make dashboards in Rolls-Royces, isn't it? That must be a lucrative crime. A single tree can net up to six thousand dollars.''

Barret Madison turned back to her, astonished. "How could you possibly know—"

"I read it somewhere," she shot back quickly, realizing how close she had to come to blowing her New York persona and revealing herself to be a dyed-in-the-wool country girl. She had to be more careful in the future, she vowed, feeling like someone who had just avoided going over a cliff by a hairbreadth.

The ticket agent came out from behind the counter carrying his keys and cash box and drew a deep, tired breath.

"Okay, okay, we can take a hint." Barret chuckled, and Vanessa liked the deep, rich sound of his mirth. "We're leaving. Is this all of your luggage, Miss Walsh?"

He indicated the two duffel bags on the floor, and Vanessa nodded. He picked one up in each hand and started for the door.

"Night, Jim," he called back over his shoulder. "Thanks for waiting."

"No problem, buddy. Good night and

drive carefully. That fog's as thick as chowder out there.''

A Jeep waiting outside the terminal door matched its owner in cleanliness. Its only mud-free areas were two quarter circles the wipers had swatted across the windshield. Barret Madison pulled open the hatchback, threw her bags inside, then bent and rubbed his jacket sleeve over the dirty taillights.

''I don't want someone rear-ending us,'' he explained as he came around to open the passenger door for her. ''Fortunately, the inside is a bit cleaner.''

He was right, she thought sarcastically as she climbed gingerly into the seat. It was a bit cleaner, nothing more. Mud, leaves, and evergreen needles coated the floor, the bench seat was covered with a wrinkled gray camp blanket, and an empty coffee cup with a half-eaten doughnut beside it sat perched precariously on the dash. It was warm and dry, however, and smelled pleasantly—familiarly for a country girl—of pine and cedar.

Outside, Barret Madison had finished polishing his headlights in a similar manner to his job on the rear ones and reached inside to retrieve the doughnut.

"I'll just get rid of that before we start," he said, and jogged around to a garbage can at the airport door. Then he hurried back to the Jeep, climbed in, and handed her the empty coffee mug. "Put that down somewhere safe, will you?" he said. "I never use the disposable kind. Environmentally devastating. There," he continued as he switched on the motor and lights. "That's better. Nice to actually be able to see where we're going."

Good grief, Vanessa thought, rolling her eyes skyward. *What kind of weirdo have I gotten myself involved with? If he and his Jeep are this unkempt, what kind of place does he live in?* Visions suddenly danced through her mind of a ramshackle cabin, its broken windowpanes stuffed

29

with rags, a woodstove oozing smoke and ash in its middle, beds with filthy striped mattresses along its sides, and a scarred plank table littered with leftover food, a single ladder-backed chair with most of its rungs missing shoved back from its head. She shuddered inwardly.

I definitely won't be tempted to do a Susan Jennings with this guy, she thought. *My only problem will be getting through two weeks in close proximity to a man who doesn't look as if he's had a bath in weeks!*

"Buckle up." He broke in on her reflections as he shifted into gear.

The drive to Barret Madison's cabin had all the elements of a dreadful dream. The fog, a real New England pea-souper, was so thick at times that Vanessa could barely see the Jeep's hood, let alone the road ahead of it. The headlights—on low beam in an attempt to focus on the road immediately before them—struggled uselessly against the heavy gossamer shroud.

Barret was silent, concentrating on his driving, and she bit her tongue each time she was tempted to ask if he knew where he was going or how much farther or how long it would take. *Best not to distract him,* she reasoned. She was immersed in this adventure well beyond the point of no return anyhow.

She fumbled in her purse and closed cold fingers around the small vial of pepper spray her mother had sent to her apartment just before she had left. It was Teddi's way of saying, ''I care. Take care.'' *I can't let her down,* she thought. *Her job may be riding on my ability to get this story and do it justice.*

She glanced over at Barret Madison, vaguely visible in the dashboard lights. His face looked strained and weary, she was startled to discover. Gone was the good-natured grin and easygoing expression he had sported in the airport waiting room. He seemed acutely alert, his expression hard and cold.

31

It's the fog, she tried to reassure herself. *Driving in this mess would stress anyone.*

A moment later, as if to reinforce her conclusions, a break in the mist revealed the road was running precariously close to a sheer dropoff unprotected by a guardrail.

She suppressed a gasp and was glad to see both of Barret Madison's strong brown hands firmly on the wheel, the booted foot at the end of his long leg close to the brake. *At least he's a competent, sensible driver,* she tried to comfort herself. *Maybe I won't die catapulting over a cliff in these mountains!*

They lurched around a final bend in the road, and in the headlights, Vanessa caught her first glimpse of a cabin built of hewn logs.

It looks capable of keeping out the elements, she thought, struggling to be optimistic. *So what if its interior is as filthy*

*as its owner. It can be cleaned . . . I know
how to clean. I only hope he has fresh
sheets . . . and soap.*

"You must be hungry," he broke in on
her reflections. He stopped the Jeep at a
side door. Vanessa caught a glimpse of a
veranda at the front before he shut off
the headlights. "There's cold chicken in
the refrigerator and butter and rolls in the
cupboard. I'll make coffee while you set-
tle in."

A few moments later he shoved open
the door, picked up her duffel bags, and
nodded for her to precede him inside.
Trying to hide her apprehension, Vanessa
complied. He followed her, shoved the
door shut with his boot heel, and snapped
on a light.

Vanessa gasped. A big, open-ceilinged
room bathed in the rich golden hue of
knotty pine walls and gleaming oak floors
sprang into view. At the rear a modern
kitchen complete with shining white ap-
pliances was separated by a varnished,

bar-style divider from the generous living room into which they had stepped. This large, open area held a long, comfortable-looking couch, several large, overstuffed armchairs, three or four rock maple tables, and two bookcases crammed to the limit with reading material. The couch faced the front of the cabin, where a huge fieldstone fireplace rose between two large windows with fawn-colored—presently drawn—drapes. She wondered if there was a lake somewhere beyond.

"There's a nice view from here," Barret Madison said, indicating the windows as if guessing her thoughts. "If you like natural beauty."

"I do," she said a bit too eagerly and quickly, and mentally reprimanded herself.

"I have a bedroom, bath, and office down there." He continued as if failing to notice her avid interest, nodding in the direction of a short corridor leading out of the room below an oak staircase that

34

gave access to the loft above. "Your sleeping quarters and bath are upstairs."

Moments later, when he had left her alone in the spotlessly clean little bedroom snuggled beneath the sloping roof at one end of the cabin, Vanessa felt like dancing in relief and delight. Although sparsely furnished with a polished pine dresser, single bed, and small night table, the room was immaculately clean and thoroughly friendly. The bed with its snowy linen and patchwork quilt looked wonderfully warm and inviting after her trip in the cold and damp. The window at the gabled end of the room even had a padded, built-in seat that appeared the perfect place to curl up with a good book or simply daydream to one's heart's content.

"It's like being back on the farm," Vanessa said to herself softly, recalling her years of growing up on her grandparents' farm in Maine while both her mother and father were off pursuing their careers.

"This situation might be tolerable after all."

With a sudden sense of abandon she threw off her suit jacket and kicked her feet free of their constricting pumps. *Tomorrow,* she thought, stretching luxuriously, *it's jeans, sweatshirt, and sneakers for this city girl.* Then she went into the compact, complete little bathroom and began to wash off her makeup. *And no more of this stuff either,* she thought triumphantly.

She was brushing her hair a few minutes later when he called to her from the foot of the stairs.

"Miss Walsh? Coffee's ready."

She came out of her room and looked down at him over the loft's polished oak railing. He was crouched before the fireplace, setting a match to the pile of logs and kindling inside. He still wore his dirty outdoor clothes and looked even more disreputable in these clean, orderly surroundings.

"You're not joining me?" she asked, remembering the half-eaten doughnut.

"I have to go out again," he said evasively as he straightened up and watched the flames leap up among the pieces of wood. "But you'll be safe. Just lock the door after me, keep the drapes drawn, and don't let anyone in no matter what. If someone does come, don't acknowledge your presence."

Vanessa felt a chill wash over her. "Where are you going? Why should I pretend I'm not here?"

"I can't go into all that," he said, turning toward her, his tone growing impatient. "As you observed on our way up here, this place is pretty isolated. I just want to make sure you're safe and warm until I get back."

"But you have electricity." Vanessa waved her hand to indicate the lights and refrigerator. "Surely—"

"A generator," he explained shortly. "If it ever happens to fail, you'll find a flashlight on your bedside table. I can assure you there are no wires connecting this place with the outside world. So please do as I ask.''

His expression was stiffening into a hard mask of stubbornness. She could see that questioning him or arguing with him at that point would do no good.

''All right.'' She feigned indifference and tripped lightly, stocking-footed, down the stairs. Stopping in front of him, she caught the earthy scent of pine and mud emanating from his clothing. She found it reassuring. It reminded her of when her grandfather had come into the big, comfortable farmhouse after working in his woodlots. ''Do you have a date?'' she asked impudently.

''I said I have to go out, okay?'' he replied shortly, turning away. ''There's pepper spray in the kitchen cupboard nearest the side door. I don't own any weapons.''

Then he opened the door, letting in a

cloud of whirling mist, and stepped outside. Seconds later the receding drone of the Jeep's motor told her he was disappearing into the mist out of which he had come.

Once the sound had died away in the distance, Vanessa walked slowly over to the door and checked the lock. Then she fell back against the panel and drew a deep breath. What kind of man had she gotten herself involved with? she wondered. Teddi had said he was a respected research biologist with no criminal record or history of any kind of social deviance. Furthermore his communications with the magazine had indicated that he was, at least at the moment, unattached romantically. Now he was dashing off into an inhospitable night like the most ardent of lovers.

Thoroughly puzzled, Vanessa went to the refrigerator and took out a golden brown chicken protected in plastic wrap. In the cupboard she found rolls and butter. As she laid the food out on the softly polished surface of the maple kitchen table and poured herself a cup of coffee, she realized she was completely ravenous and utterly exhausted. The trip from New York had been a tedious milk run of changing planes and running between closely timed flights. She determined to put all problems aside while she ate and slept. Tomorrow would be time enough to start unraveling the mystery that was Barret Madison.

She was munching on a drumstick only a few minutes later, however, when an ugly possibility raised its head to shatter that commitment. Bits of Barret Madison's conversation with the airport manager leaped back into her mind like an ugly, wart-covered toad. Timber poachers who worked at night! Timber poachers who would be muddy and carry the scent of trees about their person! The chicken leg tumbled, half-eaten, back onto the plate.

Chapter Three

Vanessa was awakened by the chattering of squirrels outside her window. She yawned and stretched, and, for a moment, was back in her old bedroom on her grandparents' farm. Then she remembered her actual situation and sat bolt upright. She had just spent an apparently peaceful night in Barret Madison's wilderness cabin.

Where was he now? she wondered. Had he come back after his mysterious departure or was she marooned here in the Canadian equivalent of an outback?

Then she became aware of the scent of coffee and toast and the sounds of movement from below. *If he hasn't returned,* she thought whimsically, *someone else must be preparing breakfast in his kitchen.*

Realizing she was hungry, she climbed out of bed, shoved her feet into her slippers, and pulled on her robe. The squirrels again scolding loudly drew her attention. She went to the window, drew aside the curtains, and broke into a smile of pure delight.

The view was breathtaking. Beyond the clearing that surrounded the cabin, modest mountains cloaked in the reds, golds, and rusts of autumn foliage rose into the clear blue sky. To the left, through the variegated leaves, she could just glimpse a lake sparkling like a huge sapphire in the morning sun.

''Oh, my!'' she said softly, enraptured. Kneeling on the window seat, she lifted the latch and opened the window to gather in a lungful of crisp, cool air.

Two red squirrels in the tree nearest her window, interrupted in their tirade by her intrusion, turned to stare at her. A moment later they scurried to a branch near the windowsill and sat up, saucily demanding a handout.

"Oh, so he feeds you, does he?" she asked, a feeling of relief washing over her. A man who provided treats for small forest creatures couldn't be all bad, she told herself.

With a tinge of embarrassment she recalled her clandestine, cursory search of his private quarters the previous evening after she had eaten. She had found nothing suspicious, however, only a very neat, very masculine bedroom and bath and an office with a computer surrounded by heaps of very scientific-looking books, papers, and handwritten notes. There had been nothing to connect Barret Madison in any way with the timber poachers.

"I'll see you later," she promised, returning her attention to the pair, and closed the window.

She paused a moment before the mirror to run a brush through her hair, and wondered how she might tactfully bring up the subject of a shower and shave to her host. A shower, at least, she compromised as she opened her door and went out onto the balcony. Perhaps the lady in his life preferred the ruggedly bearded type, and, if so, that, given his mad rush last evening to be with her, would definitely rule out a shave. At the head of the stairs, however, surprise stopped both her and her musings short.

Below in the kitchen area a man she knew had to be Barret Madison was taking golden brown bread from the toaster. She knew it had to be her story subject from his hair color, build, and height. Aside from those features, however, the man making breakfast bore little resemblance to the dirty, unkempt person she had met the previous evening.

Freshly shaved and with his thick, sun-streaked hair still damp from a shower, Barret Madison—bathed in sunlight streaming in through the window over the sink—looked every inch the male-model-handsome creature whose photo had gotten him chosen as a ''Could You Marry This Man?'' feature.

Wow! she thought, then instantly checked herself.

''Good morning,'' she said, struggling to hide her surprise and resume her cool New York persona.

''Good morning,'' he replied, turning to flash a gleaming smile up at her. ''Sleep well?''

She was glad to see that the dirty clothes he had worn the previous night were gone. He was dressed in a blue sweatshirt, well-fitted jeans, and rugged-looking hiking boots. He would have been a fitting subject for any of the sportswear ads she had become so familiar with during her weeks in her previous position in New York. *More than fitting,* she thought.

Then she became aware of his returning her interest and felt a hot blush spreading over her. His gaze was ranging over her with the beginnings of amusement, and she was intensely aware of her nose-to-toes flannelette housecoat and pajamas.

"Very well," she replied, trying not to look as discomfited as he was making her feel. "Did you . . . after you came in?"

"Like a log," he said, ignoring her mild attempt at questioning his absence and making her flinch inwardly at the thoughts his casual use of imagery had evoked in her mind. "How about an omelet?"

"Sounds great. Do you need help or may I jump into the shower?"

"Jump," he said.

"Thanks," she replied, turning back into her room. "I'll do the washing up."

Uh-oh, she thought as she turned on the water in the shower and adjusted the temperature. *He's changed! It's like a metamorphosis or something! And what's even more surprising, we were as companionable as cheese and crackers just now. I'd better get a grip. Remember Teddi and the promise.*

When she joined him for breakfast fifteen minutes later, she wore jeans, sneakers, and a navy sweatshirt, *Property of the City of New York* scrawled across the front. Her hair was soft and bright from a shampoo and blow-dry, her face fresh and free of makeup. As she sat down at the table and he placed a western omelet and toast before her, she felt so much at home she had to give herself another mental reprimand.

"Coffee?" he asked, bringing a pot toward the table, a smile Vanessa had to

49

fight not to find completely devastating warming his ruggedly handsome face.

"Yes, please. Mr. Madison, it really isn't necessary to treat me like a guest. I can take care of myself." She picked up a piece of toast and bit into it with a sharp crunch.

"Really?" He grinned wickedly, sitting down across from her with a similarly full plate. "I thought I detected just a wee bit of apprehension last night when I told you I had to go out and leave you alone."

"I was surprised." She was too quick to defend herself, immediately realized it, choked a little on her toast, and was annoyed. "It wasn't exactly what I'd expected. You'd given the editor at the magazine the impression you were unattached."

"Ah, so that's it." He paused, a forkful of omelet on its way to his mouth. Slowly he replaced the food on his plate and leaned back in his chair. "Well, maybe

I'd better tell you the truth about those letters. I didn't write them.''

"What?'' Vanessa almost choked again, this time on the coffee she had been sipping.

"The letter and all ensuing correspondence were hoaxes, a colossal prank Jeff Winston, one of the park rangers, played on me. Now don't look so stricken.'' He held up a restraining hand as she threatened to leap to her feet. "I fully intend to let you get your story. I only want you to understand that I'm not so shallow as to want to display myself in that male supermarket your editor calls a regular column.''

"If you have such a low opinion of the column, then why are you going along with it?'' she said, feeling herself growing hot from shame and beginning to tremble with outrage.

"Because you were already on your way by the time Jeff let me in on what he'd done,'' he replied. "Since he brings my mail from town, it was easy for him to intercept any correspondence from your publication until it was too late. Even that picture he submitted was a scam . . . something he and I did one day after he'd read that 'Could You Marry This Guy' feature in an old issue of your magazine a tourist had forgotten at the ranger station. He bet me I couldn't make myself look irresistible enough to warrant a feature. And since I'm not one to ignore a challenge, I let him take a few pictures. I never imagined he'd let things get to this point.''

As he talked, Vanessa had felt herself shrinking inwardly. The victim of a practical joke on her one chance to make good. At the moment it didn't matter that it had been her mother who had actually been deceived.

''Hey, don't look like that!'' He picked up the coffeepot and offered to replenish her cup.

Mutely she shook her head. Words

wouldn't form above her constricted, bone-dry throat.

"We'll do the story," he continued, filling his own cup. "Jeff's bizarre sense of humor won't be the reason for you to lose work. And what's more, we'll make me so completely irresistible your editorial offices will be flooded with mail from fascinated females." He flashed a crooked, good-natured grin at her across the table.

His compassion was more than she could bear. Snatching up a slice of toast, she jumped to her feet and rushed up to her room.

Fifteen minutes later she heard him coming almost cautiously up the stairs. "May I come in?" he asked outside her closed bedroom door.

"It's your house," she replied sullenly from her place on the window seat, and went back to feeding bits of toast to the two squirrels perched on the sill.

The door opened slowly and she could

sense his tall, masculine presence entering as she kept her back stubbornly turned to him.

"Look, I'm really sorry," he said as a soft squeak indicated he had seated himself on the edge of her freshly made bed. "Jeff's a great guy, but sometimes he lets his sense of humor get out of hand. Now the only way to foil a practical joker is to let the air out of his plans. We can do that by going ahead with the article as coolly and professionally as if it had all been our idea. What do you say?"

Silhouetted in the sunlight streaming in through the window, she turned to face him.

"You'd be willing to do that?"

"Sure," he said. "The publicity your story can give my efforts to save the park can only help. And once you get to know me better, you'll realize I'm not a passive man. No one gets the better of me. Not without a good run for his money, anyway."

The expression in his steel gray eyes told Vanessa he spoke the truth. The idea started a little shiver of excitement deep inside her slender body.

"Well then . . . okay." She faltered at first, then finished with conviction. She was not a passive woman either, she thought boldly.

"Great!" He arose and started for the door. "I'm taking a canoe across the lake to photograph a rare plant before the frost destroys it. Can you be ready in twenty minutes? I think you'd enjoy the trip."

"Yes," she said with sincerity. "I'd like to go with you."

One of the squirrels jumped brazenly forward at that moment and tried to snatch the remaining bit of toast from her fingers.

"Don't be greedy, Tosh," she said, breaking it in two and giving one piece to each.

"Tosh?" he asked, turning back in surprise.

"I named them Mac and Tosh," she said, suddenly feeling foolish. "Do you remember the cartoon Mac and Tosh? I'm not sure if they were squirrels or chipmunks, though."

"Hey, one of my favorite childhood memories!" He surprised her with his enthusiasm. "Great choices. I never did get around to naming them. See you in a few minutes."

He paused again, however, in the open doorway and turned back to her.

"Do you know what you reminded me of just now, sitting by that window feeding the squirrels with the sunlight glowing on your hair?"

Slowly, almost apprehensively, she shook her head.

"Snow White," he said a little sheepishly. "Surrounded by her little forest creatures in the cottage of the Seven Dwarfs."

"And are you the huntsman commissioned by the wicked queen to lose me in

56

the forest?'' His lighthearted banter was contagious, she realized, beginning to feel better.

"No,'' he said, his tone deflating. "Right now I feel a lot more like one of the dwarfs . . . the one named Dopey.''

He turned again, and this time he left, leaving a fleeting impression of unbridled virility and warmth as he closed the door.

Definitely not Dopey, she thought. *The huntsman, maybe.* She would have to wait and see on that count. But Prince Charming? Definitely too close for comfort.

That was the problem, she realized as she closed the window and arose. He was too nice, too charming. This altruism, this downright gentlemanly niceness was almost more than she could bear. Why couldn't he have been cold or distant or, better still, vain as a peacock, like Wade Johnson?

I will not like you, Barret Madison. I will not, she repeated over and over in her

57

mind as she rummaged through her suit-case for a nylon shell and tilly hat. And she wished he would suddenly become grasping and selfish and totally narcissis-tic. Then she would have no problem at all keeping her promise!

Chapter Four

Twenty minutes later they were gliding across the mirror-smooth lake, the prow of their canoe slicing through the water like scissors through cellophane. All around the lake, low mountains, their sides a potpourri of golds, greens, reds, and russets, rose into the azure blue of a cloudless autumn sky. A pair of loons that had been swimming leisurely toward them suddenly called heartily and then dived beneath the surface.

Vanessa took a deep breath and stopped paddling for a moment to allow herself to soak in the pristine beauty of it all. The morning air, crisp and hinting of an earlier frost, was warming, and she laid her paddle across the gunwales to remove her life jacket and tilly so she could pull off her now too-warm nylon jacket.

"For a New York City girl, you seem to know a lot about how to dress for wilderness canoeing," Barret said, also pausing. "Layers, tilly hat, nylon shell . . . have you done this before?"

"Yes," she replied, turning from the waist to look back at him and ask innocently, "Have you?"

"Okay, okay, point taken." He chuckled. "You're the interviewer; I'm the non-prying subject." He took up his paddle once more and dipped deep into the clear water, sending the canoe gliding forward.

"But you realize," he continued teasingly, "your reticence serves only to intrigue me. Now I'm really curious about your mysterious past."

Vanessa pretended to ignore him. She

62

plunged her paddle a bit more violently than necessary into the lake with a resultant splash.

"Oops! Sorry!" She feigned innocence as icy water flew back over her companion and he yelped in surprise. "I guess I'm not as good at this canoeing thing as you thought."

His reply was a muted chuckle.

Mysterious past indeed, she thought as they moved forward again. Wasn't it supposed to be the man who possessed such an alluring attribute?

"Look to your right," he said after a few minutes of silence. She did and gasped. A side of mountain previously hidden by a small island in the lake had come into view. Denuded of trees, scarred with ragged stumps and heaps of browning brush, rutted roads and crooked drains crisscrossing its face, its entire height had been devastated by clear-cut logging.

"Good heavens!" she said softly. "Is that allowed in a provincial park?"

"Big business." He shrugged. "Power. Money. The only way it can be stopped—maybe—is if I can prove there are some unique plants and animals in this area that will become extinct if logging isn't prohibited once and for all. As the situation stands, the spawning areas in the brooks near the base of that mountain have been destroyed. Sand and silt have washed down its bare sides into the water, covering the gravel beds where brown brook trout, indigenous to this area, normally deposit their eggs."

"That's terrible!" Vanessa said. "Is this all because of those bird's-eye maple poachers the airport manager mentioned to us last night?"

"No," he replied, gesturing toward the ravaged mountainside. "Sadly, that's all perfectly legal—government licensed and all . . . so far. The men who steal bird's-eye maple pick only those special trees with the valuable pockmarked core. It's a

64

highly profitable, if slightly risky, undertaking.''

"Slightly risky?" Vanessa stopped paddling and turned once more to face him, surprised. "Surely the park rangers—"

"Are few and far between, too spread out in their patrols to be much of a danger to crafty woodsmen who scout by day and butcher by night. I'll show you some of their handiwork before you leave."

They had almost reached the shore toward which they were headed when Vanessa caught her breath in sheer delight. Just ahead a beautiful doe had stepped cautiously out of the bush. Thrilled, Vanessa stopped paddling. The ensuing silence told her her companion had as well. As the canoe drifted slowly and silently toward shore, the lovely creature stood rock-still, gazing at the equally unmoving figures in the boat.

Suddenly there was a harsh, urgent snorting and crashing in the trees behind the little animal. Instantly the doe whirled and, tail held high to reveal its warning white underside, leaped gracefully out of sight into the alders. More noises in the bushes indicated her flight with another creature.

"She wasn't long answering his call," Vanessa said, her tone reflecting annoyance.

"His?" Barret asked. "You knew she was responding to a buck?"

"Wasn't it obvious?" she asked.

"Probably not to most women born and brought up in New York City," he said.

"Who said anything about being born and brought up in New York City?" She was quick to squelch his second attempt at questioning that morning. "By the way, where were you born and brought up, Mr. Madison?"

"Touché!" He laughed heartily. "You're a challenge, Miss Vanessa Walsh. You checkmate me at every turn and intrigue me doubly each time you do it. I think the next two weeks are going to be great fun.''

Vanessa dipped her paddle and propelled the canoe up onto the shore with a quick, hard stroke. She hoped the hot blush she felt suffusing her body was not visible at the back of her neck. So the next two weeks were going to be great fun, were they? She would see about that!

Together and without further conversation, they got out of the canoe and beached it high and dry. Then Barret shouldered a backpack he had brought from the canoe and led the way through the alders and up a slight incline into a small clearing accented by rocks and boulders. Tough-looking little green plants and mosses struggled out between these inhospitable formations.

''It's called Bigalow's Sedge,'' he said, kneeling and pulling aside some of the taller bushes to reveal a ragged little plant huddling beneath. ''It's been around since the last ice age but has only managed to survive here in the park. Its unique presence may be the key to saving this entire area from the devastation of logging.''

''That's wonderful!'' Vanessa said, kneeling beside him to examine the scrubby greenery. ''Do you think you can make a sufficiently strong case to influence the government?''

''I have to,'' he said, opening the backpack and taking out a Nikon camera. ''Otherwise this whole area will look like that mountainside I showed you, and these beautiful, pristine lakes will become merely dirty, lifeless sludge ponds.''

Vanessa fell silent and watched as he snapped photo after photo of the strange little plant. He rolled first this way and then that to get as many different angles as possible until he was coated with twigs and leaves. His intense dedication impressed her almost as much as his total lack of concern for his appearance did. She longed to burst out her own enthusiasm for his project and her desire to help.

Oh, right, a sarcastic voice in the back of her mind sneered. *Help him, roll around in the leaves with him, why don't you? That would be really metropolitan of you, Vanessa.*

He sat up then, put the camera aside, and, pulling a notepad and pencil from his backpack, proceeded to make notes. Vanessa sat quietly to one side, not wanting to break his concentration and trying desperately not to think how handsome he was with the sunlight on his light brown hair, thoughtful crinkles forming between his eyebrows as he wrote.

"Bored?" he asked, finally closing his book and putting away the pencil. He flashed her a smile as he got to his feet and brushed leaves from his pants and sweater.

"Not in the least," she said, squinting up at him in a shaft of sunlight that had sliced through the trees. "It's beautiful here."

"Yes, it is, isn't it? But beautiful or not,

I've got work to do. Come on. It's well over a mile's hike to my next site. Think you're up to it, or do you want to wait with the canoe?'' He held out a strong brown hand in an offer to help her up.

''Of course I'm up to it.'' She hesitated only a moment before accepting his hand. The instant his warm fingers closed over hers, however, she felt an involuntary shock wave tingle from the point of contact to the very heart of her solar plexus.

To add to her inner turmoil, he was smiling down at her, the crinkles at the corners of his devastating gray eyes complementing those at the ends of his sensuous mouth. *Oh, great,* the little voice sneered. *Turn to jelly at his slightest touch. Is that cold, sophisticated professionalism or what?*

She almost vaulted to her feet then and quickly withdrew her hand.

''Thanks,'' she said, brushing off the seat of her jeans and hoping her voice didn't sound as high-pitched and unnatural to his ears as it did to hers. "Let's go."

"Great," he said, gathering up his camera and slinging his pack onto his back. "We're off."

Apparently he wasn't similarly incapacitated, she thought, as they started off down a narrow, overgrown trail. *Terrific! All you have to worry about is controlling your own silly emotions.*

Late in the afternoon they began hiking back to the canoe. It had been a wonderful day, Vanessa thought. Barret's extensive knowledge of forests, lakes, and streams had enthralled her. She felt she had learned more about flora and fauna in the past few hours than she had learned in all of her high school biology classes.

Moreover, it had been a completely comfortable day. Vanessa had not realized how tiring Wade's constant flow of sharp, often caustic repartee had been until she had spent a day with Barret Madison. She had never been able to relax

71

with Wade or really enjoy talking with him, she thought. They had had no common interests aside from journalism, and even there Vanessa had felt less than adequate in discussions with Wade. His ethics had come nowhere near hers; once he had even called her an idealistic prude.

Suddenly she smiled. That would be the last time Wade Johnson's memory would cloud her sky. In that moment, following Barrett Madison's broad-shouldered form down a pristine wilderness footpath with the light of a setting sun silhouetting the man guiding her, Vanessa Walsh knew she was finally her own woman again.

Barret Madison. She smiled coyly to herself as she stepped over a protruding root. He was something else entirely. Interesting, intelligent, and interested in so many things. He had shown her the devastation caused by poachers who had cut large slices from the sides of sugar maples, only to discover they were not of the bird's-eye variety. He had told her about

72

logging contracts granted to big business, and how they could lead to the eventual destruction of this area that had never yet been settled or violated in any way.

He had talked about moose and deer and bears and butterflies and mice. And he had listened intently to every comment Vanessa had made and commented appropriately. He gave respect as readily as he inspired it, Vanessa realized. That would be a great opening line for her story, she thought, delighted at her inspiration.

"You've got yourself a bit of a sunburn," he said, as they straightened from launching the canoe a few minutes later.

He touched the tip of her pink nose with a gentle finger and smiled. Vanessa looked up into those gray eyes, now as soft and gentle as a summer cloud, and felt the beginnings of the thing she had promised her mother—her boss—to avoid at all costs. Quickly she turned away and jumped into the canoe.

"Tomorrow I'll wear more sun-

73

screen,'' she replied as coldly as she could manage with her heart racing.

As they crossed the lake, Vanessa saw a dark green truck parked beside Barret's Jeep near the cabin. A tall, slender man in a tan uniform stood on the shore at the canoe landing site. When they came near, he waved and called out.

''Hey, Barry! I wondered where you were. Off cataloging more of our wilderness for posterity, were you?''

''Something like that,'' her companion said, and gave a deep, hard thrust with his paddle, which sent the canoe lunging forward until its nose had glided with a soft crunch up onto the sandy beach.

The stranger grabbed the prow and gave it a powerful pull that brought the craft still farther ashore to allow both passengers to alight without getting their feet wet.

''Miss Walsh, this is Jeff Winston, otherwise known as the perpetrator.'' Barret briefly introduced her to the pleasant-looking young man who was holding out a hand to assist her from the canoe. "He's assistant superintendent of this park. Jeff, this is Vanessa Walsh."

"I'm glad to meet you," Jeff Winston said as she accepted his offer and climbed out to stand on the shore beside him. "I hope you're enjoying your visit and Barret isn't being too bearlike."

"Bearlike?" she asked.

"He's referring to an ancient derivation of Barret that means bearlike." Barret scowled at his friend. "Just can't leave me alone, can you, Ranger Rick?"

"Now he's baiting me." Jeff laughed. "As you can see, Miss Walsh, we've got a running battle of wits going. Too bad Barry sometimes runs low on ammunition."

Vanessa laughed. She had been prepared to dislike Jeff Winston, the practical joker whose prank had brought her up here on a ruse, but found she couldn't.

"My name means *butterfly,*" she retorted. "Maybe someday I'll live up to it and actually try my wings, symbolically speaking."

"Can you stay for supper, Jeff?" Barret asked, securing the canoe and confirming Vanessa's impression of the two men's friendship.

"I was counting on it," he said. "I've got a cooler with potato salad, cold roast beef, and a bottle of red wine in the truck. A sort of peace offering to you both."

"What do you say, Vanessa? Are we ready to forgive and forget?" Barret winked at her and she felt a pleasant warmth spread over her at his implied complicity.

"I guess we can be magnanimous just this once," she said. "Besides, I'm starving, and ripe for taking a food bribe of almost any kind." She removed her hat, laid it on the canoe seat, and fluffed her hair with her fingers.

"Is that to say you don't especially care for my offering?" Jeff asked as

Barret slung his backpack over his shoulder and the three started for the cabin.

"Actually, roast beef and potato salad are among my favorite foods," she said.

"That's right, Jeff, win her over with food and wine," Barret said sarcastically, going up onto the wide veranda and opening the front door. "Cover up what a blackguard you really are."

Jeff laughed and turned back to his truck to get the cooler.

"I like him," Vanessa said, as they entered the cabin, which felt chilly after the warmth of the autumn sun.

"So do I," Barret replied. "Jeff's a great guy even if—" He stopped abruptly and Vanessa looked up at him sharply.

"Even if what?" she asked.

"Nothing," he said shortly. "Let's set the table."

Chapter Five

"That was great." Barret leaned back in his chair away from the table. "I'll get the coffee."

"No, let me," Vanessa said, rising. "You two start a fire." She shivered. "It's chilly now that the sun has gone down."

"Good deal." Jeff got up and headed for the side door. "Let's get some wood, Barry."

They went out and Vanessa busied herself putting their few dishes and cutlery in the sink and bringing a tray with cups and a percolator to the table in front of the fireplace.

She waited a few minutes, and, when they failed to return, went to the door to see what was detaining them. Through the screen she saw the two men near the woodpile in the gathering dusk facing each other, obviously deep in serious conversation. Surprised, she retreated into the shadows and listened.

"Come on, Barry, it's only a few bucks," Jeff was saying. "You can afford it. And this will be the last time."

"Jeff, you said that last week," Barret said, annoyance coloring his tone. "And the week before that. It's got to end."

"Damn it, Barry! I need that money! I have to get out of this backwater once in a while and have some fun. I'm not a Grizzly Adams type like you! I don't enjoy spending every waking minute in the bush. And I haven't got a gorgeous girl like Tracey or that New York reporter in there to come back to at night. Give me a break!''

''Vanessa's hardly enamored of me,'' Barret said shortly. ''But okay. One last time.'' He pulled his wallet from his back pocket and handed his friend a few bills. ''I'll have to write you a check for the rest when we get back inside. Just follow my lead when I explain in front of Vanessa.''

''Thanks, Barry,'' Jeff said, pocketing the money. Then, together, they bent over the woodpile to gather up armfuls of wood.

Vanessa hurried back to seat herself nonchalantly in front of the fireplace. When they returned she was pouring herself a cup of coffee.

''Before you leave, Jeff, I'll write you a check to cover the cost of those supplies you bought for me last week,'' Barret was saying as they entered.

''Thanks, buddy,'' Jeff, putting his wood into the box by the fireplace. His sense of relief was obvious in his face as he knelt to put an old newspaper, kindling, and a couple of logs into the hearth and Barret went toward his office.

"You buy supplies for Mr. Madison?" Vanessa couldn't help questioning.

"Sometimes." Jeff glanced furtively at her and then went back to building a fire. "Barry has a tendency to become something of a hermit once he settles in here. He doesn't want to come to town any more than is absolutely necessary."

Then Barret was back and handing Jeff a small slip of paper Vanessa recognized as a check. His face held an expression of deep concern.

"Thanks, Barry." Jeff's tone conveyed a sense of relief and sincerity.

"Take care, my friend," Barret said, and slapped him companionably on the back. "Just take care."

"Yeah, sure." Jeff threw a match into his carefully prepared pile of paper, kindling, and wood and arose. "I'd better get going. It's a long drive to town. Good night, folks.''

When the ranger had gone, the biologist stood staring thoughtfully after him through the screen door. Only after the truck's lights had vanished into the darkness down the trail did he turn back to Vanessa and shut the inside door.

"Is something wrong?" she asked, as he started slowly back into the living room.

"No . . . no." He pulled himself out of his pensive mood. "May I have some of that coffee? As you said, it's cold in here, and it will take a few minutes for the fire to ease the chill."

For a few minutes they drank their coffee in silence, both lost in private thoughts. Then Barret arose and began closing the drapes.

"Hey!" Vanessa was indignant. "I was enjoying watching night falling over the lake and mountains."

"I can't let the cabin lights be a beacon

85

to anyone traveling through the bush,'' he said shortly, and his tone sent a little chill of apprehension washing through her. ''It could be dangerous.''

''Why? What are you afraid of?'' she asked.

''There are timber poachers in these woods, men who work at night and aren't afraid of doing a little violence for the high profits they're after,'' he said, going to close the curtains on the window over the kitchen sink. ''I don't want them stumbling across this cabin and feeling threatened by its occupants.''

Without further explanation, he went down the short hallway and into his bedroom. Vanessa hugged herself and rubbed her upper arms with her hands in an effort to dispel the tremor building inside her slender body.

What was Barret Madison up to? What was the real reason he felt compelled to give the ranger money? Why had he found it necessary to concoct a story to explain it to her? And the most torturous question of all, who was Tracey and what part did she play in Barret Madison's life? She looked into the crackling flames and tried to reassure herself that nothing could be seriously wrong. After all, Teddi had checked him out, hadn't she?

As for the mysterious Tracey, what difference did it make if Barret Madison was somehow involved with her? Vanessa would simply omit that fact from her story and let him appear the height of eligibility to her readers.

Five minutes later, however, he brought all her apprehensions crashing back as he stepped out of his bedroom clad as he had been on their first meeting, in grungy bush clothes and a battered hat. Startled, Vanessa closed the book she had been trying to read and turned in her place on the couch to stare at him.

"You're going out . . . again tonight?" she asked.

"Yes," he said, avoiding her gaze.

"To see a woman?" Vanessa couldn't stop herself from questioning boldly.

He had started for the door, but at her question he paused, hesitated a moment, and then turned back to face her.

"Yes . . . to see Tracey," he said, looking directly at her, his expression as unreadable as a blank sheet of paper.

"Is she pretty?" Vanessa was distressed to hear herself shamelessly pursuing the subject and equally disturbed by the strange sinking feeling in the pit of her stomach.

"Pretty? Yes, you could call her pretty," he said, buttoning up his dirty jacket.

"You seem very casual about a woman you dash out to meet night after night," she pressed, unable to stop herself, yet disgusted by her need to know.

"I'm hardly dashing." He continued across the room and paused with his hand on the doorknob.

"Yet you must be in love with her."

Vanessa was ashamed of her questioning but could not contain her raging curiosity.

"Love!" he scoffed, turning back toward her. "Hardly. Tracey Coldwell is best described as an obligation, in my vocabulary."

"Well, aren't you just too romantic for words!" Vanessa could no longer control her outrage.

"Look, I never said I was God's gift to women," he said bitterly. "And furthermore, I don't plan to discuss my relationship with Tracey with anyone. I have to go now. Keep the drapes drawn, lock the door, and don't let anyone in or acknowledge your presence in the cabin. Do you remember where the pepper spray is?"

"Yes," she snapped. "I'll be fine. Remember, I'm a big girl from the big city. Give Tracey my best regards. She probably needs them. She doesn't seem to have yours!"

"Ahhhhh . . . !" Thoroughly annoyed,

89

he yanked open the door and let in a gust of cold night air. ''Remember, don't let anyone in!'' he threw back over his shoulder as he strode out and slammed the door on his last word.

''Don't worry, Dopey!'' she yelled after him. ''I'm not about to let the wicked queen get me with a poison apple!''

Leaving the coffee things where they were, Vanessa snapped off the lights. In the flickering glow of the dying fire she stamped angrily up to bed.

Two hours later, although cozily ensconced in her bed with a good book, Vanessa was feeling miserable. She wished they hadn't parted on such a bitter note. After all, who was she to question his comings and goings? He'd been understanding and generous in granting her a story even though he too had been duped by Jeff Winston's practical joke. The problem was entirely hers. She had let herself get personally involved. Now she might have blown the whole thing.

She decided she would wait up for him and apologize. There was nothing else she could do. . . .

She awoke with a start. A glance at her bedside clock told her it was nearly 4:00 A.M. Her book lay where it had fallen from her hands and her lamp was still on. She grimaced as she remembered her resolve to wait up for Barret. But what had awakened her now?

Then a sound below brought her to full alert. Had he returned? Remembering his warnings, however, she snapped off her light before going cautiously to ease open her door. In the kitchen area she was relieved to see Barret getting a glass of water at the sink.

"Mr. Madison?" she said cautiously as she advanced to the railing. "Are you all right?"

He turned to face her, glass in hand,

and she was astounded at how haggard he looked. His jacket and pants were filthy, his boots caked with mud.

"Go back to bed," he said gruffly.

"Are you all right?" she repeated, concerned.

"Yes, yes." He dismissed her with a wave of his hand.

"I just wanted to tell you I'm sorry for what I said earlier," she said hesitantly. "I hope you and Tracey had a pleasant evening."

"I'd hardly call it pleasant," he said, sinking into a chair at the kitchen table and stretching long legs out beneath it. "But thanks." He looked up at her and grinned wanly. "I'm sorry too."

"Good night," she said, and went back into her room.

She felt a little better as she settled into bed. Yet she was still concerned and confused. Why would a man come home from a date, even a casual, unenthusiastic one, looking so unhappily exhausted?

92

What was the state of his relationship with the mysterious Tracey?

The next morning, as a result of her broken rest, she did not awaken until after eight o'clock. When a quick perusal of the main floor told her he was not yet stirring, she treated herself to a leisurely shower and blow-dried her hair. There was something to be said for an expensive New York color and styling job, she decided as she finished. It made your hair look great with a minimum of effort. She liked that. Fussing with an elaborate hairdo had never been her forte. Nor had makeup or fancy dresses or . . . Suddenly she found herself wondering what Tracey looked like. Was she pretty, sophisticated, maybe even glamorous? Whatever Tracey Coldwell was, Vanessa ended her musings with a sigh, she definitely had the power to devastate Barret Madison utterly and completely.

Dressed for the outdoors in a plaid flannel shirt, jeans, and hiking boots, Vanessa went downstairs quietly and tried to shove all speculation about Barret and Tracey from her mind. She found coffee and plugged in the percolator. Then she rummaged in the cupboards and discovered pancake mix. A bowl of apples sitting on the kitchen counter inspired her, and she decided to make apple pancakes with cinnamon topping, one of her grandmother's best breakfasts. She was searching the cupboards for cinnamon when his voice stopped her.

"Good morning," he said, and she turned to face him as he came into the kitchen area wrapped in a blue calf-length terry robe, below which his feet and legs were bare. He was unshaven, his hair tousled from sleep, but he set Vanessa's pulses racing. The words *sexy, virile, natural, earthy, completely irresistible* galloped across her mind.

"Good morning," she replied desperately, hoping her thoughts didn't show in her expression. "I didn't expect you to be up until noon."

"I can't let my nocturnal ramblings interfere with my work," he said, scratching his head and yawning. "I'm a working biologist, you know."

"I was just about to make apple-cinnamon pancakes." Vanessa bit back a caustic comment about his referring to his date with Tracey as *nocturnal rambling* and forced a smile. "Would you like some?"

"I would love some." He yawned. "May I jump into the shower while you prepare that wonderful feast? I'll wash up today."

"Jump," she said.

Ten minutes later the pancakes were spread out on a cookie tray to keep warm in the oven when Vanessa realized her tilly hat was missing. *Darn,* she thought. *I'll need it when we go out today.*

She recalled she had last seen it when she and Barret had been beaching the canoe the previous day. Had she left it down by the lake? she wondered. She would take a quick look while she was waiting for Barret to join her.

Sure enough, she thought jubilantly a few moments later as she picked up the hat, damp with a heavy near-frost dew, from beside the beached canoe. She turned to go back to the cabin. And froze.

Directly between herself and the cabin, a huge black bear stood staring at her.

Chapter Six

The bear was slavering, its wide sides heaving. It looked more confused and disoriented than threatening. Vanessa tried to calm her racing heart. Yet one could never tell with a bear.

Avoiding eye contact, she began to edge her way slowly around it. When she was almost past it, the animal grunted and moved suddenly, as if about to charge. With a sharp flick of her wrist, she flung the hat she was carrying toward it and burst into a run toward the cabin.

Barret, naked except for a towel

99

wrapped about his hips, burst out of the cabin as she scrambled up the steps. Grabbing her arm, he pulled her roughly inside.

''Good Lord!'' he said, slamming the door shut behind them. ''How did you get into that mess with Buster?''

''Buster?'' She gasped, falling back against the wall in an effort to catch her breath. ''Buster? You mean that bear is another of your furry forest friends? I must say, I prefer Mac and Tosh.''

''Well, sort of a nodding acquaintance,'' he said, slowly releasing his grip on her arm. ''He comes to the lake most mornings to fish, but he generally stays a respectable hundred and fifty yards or so upshore. What he's doing in the yard today I don't know. I believed we had an understanding. Are you sure you're okay?'' he asked as she walked over to the couch and sank down into it to fan herself with a shaky hand.

''Me? Oh, sure, certainly. Why should

100

coming face-to-face with a four-hundred-pound omnivore before breakfast bother me?'' She glanced sarcastically over at him.

''Glad to see you haven't lost your sense of humor.'' He grinned, sitting down in the armchair across from her and not seeming to care that he was dripping wet, his hair slicked back like a greaser from the fifties. ''But what are you grinning about?'' he continued. ''I can't say I find the incident all that amusing.''

''Were you planning to take Buster on bear-to-bare?'' She suppressed a chuckle, pointing at the towel. ''Pun definitely intended.''

''Laugh if you like,'' he said, getting up and suddenly looking self-conscious. ''But when I glanced out the bathroom window and saw you and Buster having a one-on-one confidence competition, I didn't feel I had time to select clothes appropriate to the situation. Forgive me if my concern for your safety lacked the proper trappings.''

He arose and started back to the bathroom. The tail of his towel flapped against his thighs in spite of his efforts to appear to be departing with offended dignity.

''Sorry, Sir Galahad.'' She stifled a giggle. ''It's just that . . . I mean, that is, aren't knights supposed to wear shining armor?''

By now he had reached the bathroom. With a lightning-swift move, he whipped off the towel, flung it into her laughing face, and vanished inside.

Five minutes later when they sat down to eat their pancakes, their eyes met as he handed her the syrup jar, and suddenly they both burst out laughing.

When their mirth had subsided, Vanessa wiped her eyes and chuckled. ''Poor Buster. I'm sure he was more upset than I. I hope he didn't eat my hat, though. It's the only one I brought with me.''

"You seem amazingly unconcerned about all this, for a city girl." Barret grew serious and poured himself coffee. "And that trick of throwing your hat for him to sniff while you made your getaway . . . where did you learn that?"

"Bears will usually stop and sniff at anything you throw in front of them," she replied nonchalantly as she helped herself to a pancake.

"I know," he said, adding cream to his cup. "But I'm surprised you do."

"Just a little more of my mysterious past," she said, and cut into the fruit-filled delicacy.

She flashed him an exaggerated co-quettish look and a long, slow wink as she raised her fork to her mouth. She knew she was deliberately pushing the myth, since it appeared to intrigue him. *Stop it,* the little voice ordered. *You're flirting outrageously and you know it.*

"Right," he said with a light dash of

103

sarcasm. ''Man, I hope these pancakes taste even half as good as they look.''

He turned his attention to cutting into one of the fluffy, golden brown cakes and ignored her bait. Vanessa felt disappointed. *That's what you get for teasing,* the voice told her.

A half hour later the cabin had been set to rights, and they were about to leave for another foray into the bush.

''Today I'll show you some of the devastation those tree poachers have caused,'' Barret said, as they packed the Jeep for what he had said would be a day-long expedition.

''I'm interested,'' she said. ''But first let me see what Buster left of my hat.''

Humming contentedly, she walked back toward the place where she had tossed her hat to the bear. She found it intact. Apparently the animal had lost interest quickly. Then she glanced up along the shoreline and stopped short.

Promise Pending

About a hundred and fifty yards up-shore Buster sat up doglike on his haunches, gazing out across the lake. He appeared relaxed and harmless, plump and ready for a comfortable winter's hibernation.

"Looks like an overgrown teddy bear, doesn't he?" Barret said, coming to join her. "And basically, given space and respect, he is. The trouble is, the human world is closing in on him. His habitat is shrinking each year, his hunting grounds are disappearing, and he's becoming easy prey for poachers who bait with food and run a despicable and illegal trade in wild animal organs and parts. I'm fond of the big lug, but I have to chase him away. He's too trusting. Here, take a good look at him."

He handed her a pair of binoculars and she took them eagerly. She loved seeing wild animals in their natural setting. Through the magnifying lenses she saw

Buster looking happy and contented. He yawned lazily and scratched his fat belly.

Suddenly a butterfly appeared and began to flutter about his ears and snout. Playfully, almost gently it seemed, he brushed it away. Shortly it was back, however, and Buster, after several more vain attempts to chase it away, dropped on all fours and ambled off into the forest. Just before he disappeared from view, however, Vanessa laughed aloud. The troublesome butterfly had lighted on his head and was hitching a ride.

''Isn't he great?'' Barret said enthusiastically as she lowered the binoculars, still chuckling.

She saw the Nikon wearing a long zoom lens in his hands. ''While you were observing, I was snapping away. I think I got a few good ones . . . some I can use to prop up my case against logging in this area. Now let's go.'' He turned and headed back toward the Jeep. ''We've got a lot of ground to cover today.''

During the remainder of the morning Barret took her on a motor tour of the park. Vanessa was enraptured by what she saw. Large, peaceful lakes at the base of multicolored mountains reflected the autumn splendor rising around them. And as they drove along the narrow road bordering one of these mountain reservoirs, gold and crimson birch and maple leaves formed a sun-dappled canopy overhead.

Several times Barret had to slow or stop in order to let partridge, rabbits, squirrels, or chipmunks cross ahead of them. Once a beautiful red fox appeared briefly on the edge of the road before darting back into cover.

''It's wonderful,'' Vanessa said, and, glancing over at Barret, she saw he was smiling at her pleasure.

''It is, isn't it?'' he said softly, and Vanessa felt her heart flutter at his deep, sincere tone. What would happen to a woman if he spoke to her, about her, like that? she wondered.

* * *

Just before noon Barret stopped the Jeep at the base of a footpath that led upward into the trees.

"How would you like to have lunch at the top of the highest peak in Atlantic Canada?" he asked. "Feel like an hour's hike . . . up?"

"Yes," Vanessa said with alacrity and opened her door. "Let's go."

Seventy-five minutes later, seated on the barren, windswept zenith of Mount Carleton, Vanessa mentally applauded her decision. The view was spectacular. Spread out around her were miles and miles of glowing autumn wilderness and pristine lakes sparkling in the sun.

"Well, what do you think of my park?" Barret asked, his use of *my* implying not ownership but deep affection as he sank down close beside her.

"Magnificent," she said. "It's like being very near to heaven."

"I agree," he said huskily.

His tone caused her to turn toward him. The expression in his gray eyes startled her. And when he made no move to glance away, she turned her attention awkwardly to some tiny red berries sprouting out of the rocky soil beside her.

"What are these?" she asked, trying to extricate herself from a situation rapidly threatening to become intimate.

She knew she must. Her pulse had struck up a mad pace, and it wasn't simply the altitude that was making her light-headed.

"They're commonly called mountain cranberries," he said, and, slowly, deliberately, leaned forward to touch his lips lightly to hers. "Now why don't you ask me their proper botanical name? That might distract me . . . for a split second."

The kiss had been as feathery and light and fleeting as the graze of a butterfly's wing . . . and just as magical. Vanessa was mesmerized. She felt as if she were drowning in a sea of gray . . . gray eyes that were warm and sincere and seductive. She had to get away, had to, had to. . . .

"Barret . . . Mr. Madison." She scrambled awkwardly to her feet and knew her cheeks were glowing. "This isn't a good idea. I . . . I'm a professional . . . writer; you're my subject. My editor warned me most specifically not to get personally involved. It could cost my job . . . and hers."

"All that serious, is it?" He squinted up at her in the sun. "Then, of course, we'll leave things just as they stand. I understand the importance of commitment to work. And I'll respect yours, if that's what you really want."

"It is," Vanessa said, hoping her words didn't sound as trembly and insincere as they felt.

"Okay." He vaulted lightly to his feet, brushed dried moss and pebbles from the seat of his jeans, and swung his pack onto his back. "We'd better go then. It's quite a hike down to the Jeep, and it gets dark early among the trees.''

When they arrived back at the cabin, the sun was setting across the lake. To Vanessa's surprise an unfamiliar gray Jeep was parked beside the cabin. Leaning against it was a slender young woman, her chestnut-colored, shoulder-length hair looking like the best from all the shampoo ads Vanessa had ever seen. Over a hunter green turtleneck she wore a saddle-colored field coat. Formfitting jeans and hiking boots completed her attire.

"Tracey," she heard Barret say in exasperation. "What is she doing here? Now?"

"She's beautiful," Vanessa said softly as they stopped a few feet from the young woman. She felt her heart sink. Had Barret actually preferred her to this lovely creature, and she, Vanessa Walsh, had turned him down?

111

"Yeah, I guess." Barret was opening his door and climbing out. He gave no hint of eagerness and offered no further explanation.

"Barret, honey, where have you been?" Tracey fairly danced around the front of the Jeep to give him a quick hug and plant a kiss on his cheek.

"Working," he replied and, after a brief hesitation, placed an almost brotherly peck on her forehead. "Why so early? I told you I'd be there at the usual time."

"Things have changed, lover," she said, slipping her arm through his and glancing mockingly across at Vanessa. "Tonight, my darling, we boogie!"

Vanessa's heart sank like a rock and landed with a hard, painful bump in the pit of her stomach. Her job wasn't worth giving up this wonderful man, she thought bitterly. If only there hadn't been Teddi and that promise to keep in mind.

Chapter Seven

Vanessa found sleep difficult that night. Immediately after their arrival back at the cabin, Barret had changed into his dirty bush gear and left with Tracey. Then he had driven off with the chestnut-haired young woman. Vanessa had felt more utterly dejected and miserable than she could ever recall having felt in her life. Wade's betrayal had been nothing compared to this, she thought.

She had found a pizza and made a half-hearted attempt at supper. Then she had

115

climbed into bed and drifted into a troubled sleep.

Suddenly she was awakened by a crash that sounded like shattering glass. Coming bolt upright in her bed, she became fully aware just in time to hear a vehicle gunning its engine in a fast retreat from the cabin yard.

A glance at the luminous hands of her clock told her it was just past midnight. Her heart thudding, she scrambled to her feet, grasped the flashlight from her bedside table, and walked softly to the door.

She eased it open and tiptoed to the loft railing. Everything was dark and silent. Gaining courage, she switched on her flashlight and swung its beam carefully about the main floor. Nothing appeared amiss until the light swept over the kitchen. There, bits of shattered glass suddenly winked up into the beam from the polished floor.

Aiming the flashlight higher, Vanessa

saw the drawn curtains above the sink trembling in the breeze, and felt a huge shiver wash over her. Someone had broken the window! Trying to still the tremor building in her slim body, she circled the room with the ray of light and saw a rock lying under the kitchen table. A crumpled bit of paper was tied to it with a string.

Her pulse and curiosity racing, Vanessa switched off her flashlight and waited for a moment until her eyes became accustomed to the darkness. Then she came cautiously down the stairs. The sound of the rapidly retreating vehicle she had heard earlier made her reasonably certain whoever had thrown the rock was gone. The intense quiet of a wilderness night had returned. Still, she was not about to rush carelessly into an ambush.

Holding her flashlight like a club in readiness, she made a quick perusal of the cabin. Both doors were still securely bolted and no other windows had been broken or forced. Reassured, she returned to the kitchen, switched on a light, and removed the note from the rock.

Madison, it read. *If you care about this park, get out before everything is destroyed. This is your last chance.*

"Oh, my Lord!" Vanessa said as she crouched in her pajamas beside the rock, the dirty sheet of paper—its words roughly cut from a newspaper—in her fingers. "Barret is one of the tree poachers!"

She remembered the money changing hands between Jeff and Barret. *Bribe money,* she thought. Paid to keep Jeff away from the areas where the stealing was taking place. She was in a den of thieves. There was no one she could trust. Lost in the awfulness of these facts, she arose, not paying attention to her movements. As she started toward the living room, she suddenly yelped in pain.

A shard of glass from the broken window had slivered into the side of her bare

118

foot. Blood was spurting out onto the hardwood floor.

"Just what I need on top of everything else," she muttered, realizing the cut was more messy than serious.

Still gripping the note, she hobbled as fast as she could back upstairs and into her bathroom, where she had seen a box of Band-Aids and gauze pads on the top shelf.

She had barely seated herself on the closed lid of the toilet and begun to stanch the flow of blood with a pad when she heard the familiar drone of Barret's Jeep motor as it approached the cabin. Her mind racing, she pressed the gauze to the cut.

What would she say when he confronted her? She looked at the crumpled note lying on the small vanity cabinet beside her. Should she hide it, take it to the authorities in the morning, or . . . ?

Her quandary was interrupted as she heard him unlocking the side door. The next moment a loud expletive told her he had seen the broken window. His next response, however, took her completely off guard.

"Vanessa!" he roared. "Dear God, Vanessa, where are you?"

Instantly he was bounding up the stairs, across the bedroom, and into the bathroom.

"Vanessa!" He pulled her from her improvised chair and into his arms. "Thank God you're all right!"

For a moment, shocked, she stood still in his embrace. Then a rush of pain from her injured foot brought her back to reality. She put her hands firmly against his broad, heaving chest and pushed herself free.

"Of course I'm okay," she said, sinking down onto the toilet lid once more. "Why shouldn't I be?"

"The window, the blood on the floor . . ." He was breathing hard, his jaw working in a nervous tic. "Who—?"

"Cowards," she said, returning her attention to her foot and trying to still the pounding his embrace had started in her heart. "They threw a rock with a note attached, then took off like bunnies with a pack of beagles on their tails. I cut my foot on the broken glass when I got carried away contemplating the note's contents."

"Contents?" he asked. "What did it say?"

Vanessa made a quick decision and pointed to the vanity. "Read it for yourself."

He picked it up, scanned the words, and muttered something derogatory under his breath.

"You've done a good job masquerading as a concerned biologist," she said contemptuously, looking up at him while she held the bandage in place. "You almost had me convinced."

"What are you talking about?" he asked.

"That note makes it all very clear," she said. "You're one of the tree poachers!"

"Me?" He was astounded and sank down to sit on the edge of the bathtub in front of her. "What made you come to that conclusion?"

"Obviously someone believes you are and wants you out of the park 'before every tree is destroyed,'" she said. "What else could it mean?"

For a moment he simply stared at her. Then he burst out laughing and dropped to his knees before her. "Here, let me do that." He chuckled, taking over the job of bandaging her foot. "You've obviously lost your senses and you're making a real mess of it. Did you check to make sure the wound is a hundred percent clean?"

"Stop it!" she cried, and tried to pull away, but he held her fast by the ankle and continued to chuckle in a completely irritating manner.

"Hold still," he ordered gently. "Let

122

me fix this foot and I'll explain . . . as much as I can, that is. Hold still, I said.''

Seeing it was useless to protest, Vanessa was forced to remain with as much dignity as she could muster on her improvised chair as he began to dress her wound.

"Explain," she said imperiously, crossing her arms stubbornly.

"Well, to begin with," he said, expertly covering the cut with gauze and beginning to tape it in place. "I'm not a timber poacher. Those people who threw the rock are the thieves. That note means that if I don't discontinue my fight to have the park protected, they'll do exactly what they've threatened to do in the past . . . set forest fires simultaneously all over the area—uncontainable fires that would devastate this region for a lifetime.''

"They wouldn't!" Vanessa gasped, appalled, her arms falling to her sides.

"They most certainly would," he said evenly, finishing his task and beginning

123

to gather up the first-aid materials scattered about the floor. "But not yet . . . not until they've stripped it of every bird's-eye maple they can find."

"And destroy countless other trees in the process," Vanessa added, gripping the edge of the toilet lid in the anger the thought of such waste had aroused in her.

"Yes," he said, pausing and looking up at her. "They definitely will."

He took her injured foot once again into his hands, but this time it was an act of caring, of tenderness. His touch made every fiber of her being turn to warm, helpless, tremulous jelly. Immediately she hated her reaction and wrenched away from him. She succeeded only in hurting herself and flinched sharply.

"Sorry," he said, turning away and beginning to gather up the first-aid supplies. "And I'm sorry, really sorry, you've been pulled into this mess. Tomorrow I'll take you to the airport and you can catch a flight to New York. It's too dangerous for you here. I should have realized that fact right away and not waited for an incident like this.''

''No! You can't send me away! I won't go! What about the story you promised me?'' Suddenly Vanessa knew she didn't want to go, desperately didn't want to go.

''Story? Haven't you been listening?'' He stood up and pulled her roughly to her feet. She flinched as her injured foot hit the cold tile, but he didn't seem to notice. ''Vanessa Walsh, I care about you. I don't want anything to happen to you. Go back to New York, write whatever you like about me. Improvise if you have to. I don't care, just so long as I know you're safe.''

Before she knew what was happening she was in his arms, his mouth coming down to cover hers in a hard, passionate kiss. His body against hers was like a stone wall, hard and unyielding, with every rippling muscle petrified with emotion. She wanted to push him away, to

125

remember her promise to Teddi, to recall Wade's ardor, which had been only a mask for self-interest. She couldn't. Barret Madison was not Wade Johnson. Barret Madison was . . . something else, a whole other ball game, and she wanted desperately to play.

Simultaneously, however, the reality of their situation burst over them. He released her and she backed free.

"Sorry again," he muttered, bending to pick up first-aid supplies from the floor. "That was a knee-jerk reaction. It won't happen again. You made our respective positions perfectly clear this afternoon."

"Well . . . well, then . . . good," Vanessa managed, although her heart and stomach were doing cartwheels. "I'll go back to bed then."

She turned and started to limp away. The next instant, however, she gasped as he swept her up into his arms. About to protest, she looked up into his tired face;

126

she saw such genuine concern mirrored there that her need to resist was instantly quelled. No one could feign such sincerity, she thought. Reassured, she accepted his kindness and allowed him to carry her into her bedroom.

Resting against the coarse fabric of his shabby coat, Vanessa felt the blatant masculine hardness of broad chest and shoulders and caught the sensuously light odor of his aftershave above the earthy smells of mud and forest that clung to his clothing. The combination was very nearly overwhelming.

Was this how Jane felt when Tarzan swept her off into the treetops, she wondered. If so, she fully understood why the jungle lord's lady never tried to escape.

When he placed her in her bed and drew the covers carefully over her, she half-expected—was wishing wildly—he would bend and, like Prince Charming, kiss her gently.

He didn't. Instead, he straightened

slowly and for a moment stood looking down at her with an expression that served only to heighten her already catapulting emotional and physical responses.

"I'd better go clean up the glass and put something over the window," he said finally, absently, his gaze still on her face. "I won't be going out again. You try to get some sleep."

"Yes," she said softly, and watched with a pounding heart as he turned and went out of the room, shutting the door softly behind him.

Later she snuggled down in the warm, comfortable bed and listened as he swept up glass and hammered something in place over the broken window, and thought, *I am not falling in love with you, Barret Madison. I am not.*

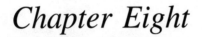

Chapter Eight

The next morning Barret drove to town to get new glass for the window and other supplies. It had begun to rain just before dawn, and while Vanessa had enjoyed its cozy patter on the roof, Barret had been less enthusiastic.

"A heavy rain at this time of year can turn the roads up here into seas of mud," he said. "I'll go to town early and stock up on supplies just in case we get marooned for a few days."

Vanessa declined his invitation to accompany him. She used her injured foot as an excuse. Actually she wanted the time to begin her story. If she were about to be sent packing, it was high time she got at it, she reasoned. She had not written a single word since she had arrived, and she was beginning to have guilt pangs. And yet somehow she felt awkward confiding in Barret that she planned to spend the day dissecting his character.

Barret had lit a fire in the fireplace. The broken window roughly patched with cardboard was letting in a chill, he declared. His concern for her comfort warmed her even more than the crackling flames in the stone hearth as she settled down in the armchair, clad in a fleece jogging suit, feet, snugly encased in woolen socks, drawn up beneath her, clipboard, paper, and pencil at the ready.

Noon, however, saw not a single thing—aside from some doodling—appear on the pad. She had sharpened her pencil twice, watched a pair of loons bobbing contentedly on the choppy, rain-pocked surface of the lake, admired the autumn foliage made more vibrant by contrast to the somberness of the day, and even several times donned rain gear and gone out to see if she could spot Buster at his fishing place. He wasn't there, but she did manage to pass a hefty block of time in the effort.

After she had come back into the cabin from her final expedition, she removed her slicker and went to one of the long windows to stare out at the mountains, their tops obscured in gossamer mist. The gray clouds reminded her of Barret's eyes . . . cold and inscrutable one moment, mysteriously sensuous the next, sparkling with silver rays of humor when, on a couple of occasions, slender shafts of sunlight tried to pierce the overcast.

She returned to the couch, sat down, drew up her knees, folded her arms across them, and rested her chin on top. *Stop it,* the voice warned her. *You're walking on thin ice now, paper-thin. Last night was a warning of what can happen if you're not careful. Take it to heart. Remember the promise. Remember how hard Teddi worked to get that job. Remember . . .*

At noon she made a pot of tea and a sandwich. Shortly after, lulled by the warmth of the fire and the patter of rain on the roof, she dozed.

She awakened with a start. The gentle rain had changed into a raging downpour that battered the shingles of the roof. Above the deluge she heard a vehicle battling its way toward the cabin, gears shifting, engine alternately gunning and relaxing as it navigated the rain-slicked trail.

Barret, she thought, jumping to her feet and instantly feeling guilty about her eagerness. She paused on her way to the door in an effort to quell her initial reaction, and a thought occurred to her. Why was he driving so strangely? Surely road conditions alone couldn't be responsible for such fitful rushes and stops, roars and calms.

The jeep halted near the side entrance and silenced. A door slammed, feet stumbled up the steps, the door burst open, and Barret half fell inside. He was dripping wet and coated with mud, but what made Vanessa catch her breath in horror was a large purple lump over his left eye.

"Barret!" she cried, rushing to take his arm as he lurched backward to close the door behind him.

"I'm okay," he muttered, but his face was ashen, his breathing rapid and shallow. "I'll be fine in a few minutes. Just have to catch my breath."

"What happened?" She gasped, feeling his weight coming against her for support, and knew he wasn't telling the truth.

"I stumbled onto the tree poachers on my way back from town," he said, putting a hand to his forehead and rubbing it as if trying to clear away the pain and

135

confusion. ''They were setting a trap for Buster on one of his paths.''

''Oh, no!'' Vanessa was appalled. She had seen bear traps when she had lived in Maine, and knew of their terrible cruelty.

''I tried to stop them . . . thought they'd run, but I guess I had them too dead to rights.'' Barret's words were becoming labored, his weight heavier on her by the second. ''One of them took an unexpected swing at me with a bit of chain from the trap. Knocked me cold. When I came to, I was lying on my back in the mud. The rain must have revived me. Anyway, they were gone and so was the trap.''

''You're shivering,'' she said softly, his courage in defending his beloved forest creatures bringing a lump to her throat. ''You have to get out of those wet clothes. Do you want me to help you?''

''Why, Miss Vanessa, ma'am . . .'' In spite of the seriousness of the situation, Barret managed to look melodramatically startled at the suggestion. "I must say, I'm . . . surprised."

"Are you sure you're really injured?" Vanessa tried to match his jesting mood, but felt herself failing as a hot blush spread up her cheeks. "Or is this just some cheap ploy?"

Her attempt at teasing failed as he slumped suddenly, completely against her and she had all she could do to keep him on his feet.

"Come on; let me help you to your bedroom," she said, gently putting an arm around his waist and letting his arm fall about her shoulders.

"Thanks," he said, the last of his bravado fading. "I need a hot shower . . . then I'll be fine."

Together they walked to the door of his room. There he paused and turned to face her, his arm still on her shoulders.

"Did anyone ever tell you you're amazing, Miss Walsh?" he said shakily.

He inclined his head and kissed her

lightly on the forehead. Then he turned and went inside, closing the door after him. Vanessa was left staring at the door blankly.

When she finally turned and walked slowly back to the living room, all she could think was, why did he have to be so darn wonderful? Greedy, nasty, self-centered she could have handled. This was entirely unfair.

When he emerged from the bedroom fifteen minutes later he had showered and put on dry clothes. His state of health showed, however, in the fact that he had left his denim shirt hanging out over his jeans and wore only gray woolen socks on his feet.

"Lie down on the couch," Vanessa said, handing him an ice pack. "Are you hungry? I made sandwiches and coffee while you were changing."

"Sounds great," he said, taking her advice and then putting the ice pack gratefully to his head. "In spite of a miserable

138

headache, I could do with some food. I haven't eaten since breakfast.''

Vanessa refrained from questioning him while he ate. He needed rest and nourishment, not a grilling. Instead she busied herself putting wood on the fire and wiping up the mud he had dripped onto the hardwood floor.

When he had finished eating she removed the dishes and took them to the sink. She was washing them when she heard him exclaim, struggle to his feet, and rush into the downstairs bathroom.

When he emerged a few minutes later he was pale and exhausted. Vanessa went quickly to his side and helped him return to the couch.

''You probably have a concussion,'' she said gently. ''That's why you're nauseated.''

''I'm fine,'' he protested, but he flinched as he sat down. ''There's no need to fuss.''

''We can't take a chance,'' Vanessa declared firmly. "You mustn't sleep . . . at least not for the next few hours. I know . . . I'll interview you. That will keep you alert."

"If it will make you happy." He sighed, sinking down more comfortably against the pillows and closing his eyes.

"No, no, no!" Vanessa shook him gently. "Don't do that! Listen to me! Pay attention! Where were you born? Who were your parents? Where did you go to school? Barret, pay attention!"

"Yes, Miss Landers," he horrified her by murmuring childishly.

"Barret!" She gasped and all but leaped on him, shaking him violently by the shoulders. He was losing touch with reality, she thought, horrified.

Chapter Nine

When her concerned face was inches above his, he opened one eye roguishly.

"Had you going there for a minute, didn't I?" He grinned crookedly.

"Turkey!" she cried, and retreated hastily. "Who was Miss Landers, anyway? An old flame?"

"My third-grade teacher," he replied. "Pretty little thing. Pity I was too young."

"Be serious." Vanessa resumed her seat in the armchair across from him and took up her pencil and clipboard.

"You've got to stay awake so that I can interview you. Barret . . . !'' she snapped as his eyes began to close again.

"Don't worry," he said, looking over at her in pretended annoyance. "I won't die before you get your story. What exactly do you want to know?"

She heaved an exasperated sigh. "Well, for starters, where were you born? What did your parents do? Why did you decide to become a wildlife biologist? What do you consider your greatest accomplishments to date?"

"Starters?" he asked, raising one eyebrow skeptically. "That's my life story."

"Come on, come on!" she pressed, thinking his eyelids were growing heavy. "You agreed."

"Yes, God help me, I did." He roused himself. "I was born in Halifax, Nova Scotia. My father is a professor of biology at the university there. My mother was a social worker until she retired last year. I have an older brother who is an engineer and a younger sister who is an emergency-room nurse.''

''A middle child, hmm?'' Vanessa chewed the top of her pencil thoughtfully.

''Now don't start psychoanalyzing me,'' he muttered. ''I'm a very straightforward person. What you see is what you get. No complexes, no secrets.''

''Right,'' Vanessa said sarcastically, beginning to write. ''What do you call dashing off into the forest night after night without even a hint of an explanation? What do you call your kinky relationship with Tracey Coldwell? What—?''

''Moving right along.'' He ignored her words, which had been heating up as they ran on. ''I decided to become a wildlife biologist because my father's work had always fascinated me. When I got my Ph.D.—''

''You're a doctor?'' Vanessa was impressed.

''Yes,'' he said with barely a break in

his narrative. "After I got my doctorate, I began to do field work for Dad. He didn't want to travel too far away from his wife and family, but he needed on-site data to complete his research." He adjusted the ice pack on his head and continued, "I believe the last question was my greatest accomplishment. Actually I hope that's yet to come, in the preservation of this great park."

"I agree." Vanessa leaned forward eagerly. "But up to this point . . . your doctorate, perhaps?"

"Definitely not. That just came along in the course of my studies." He closed his eyes for a moment as if in pain, then opened them wide and shook his head.

"Are you sure you're all right?" she asked, concern heavy in her tone. "I'm a good driver. I can take you to a doctor in town."

"I'm perfectly okay." He cleared his throat and pulled himself up to a more upright sitting position. "Go on."

146

"Well . . ." She glanced back over her notes. "This probably isn't your first field research assignment. Tell me about the others."

"Nothing much to tell," he said. "No amazing discoveries or scientific break-throughs anywhere among them."

"Well, at least give me their locations." Vanessa was growing exasperated. She needed something to flesh out her story.

"Well . . ." He adjusted the ice pack again and flinched as he touched the bruise. "The first one was in Honduras . . . a study of bird life. Parrots and toucans, to be exact."

"You lived in the jungle?" Vanessa leaned forward, instantly intrigued. "Now we're getting somewhere. For how long?"

"A few months," he said casually.

"Wasn't it dangerous?"

He shrugged. "You have to stay alert. But the jungle can be as beautiful as it is

147

deadly. Imagine a huge flock of parrots, their plumage as bright and variegated as a rainbow, coming in at sunset to roost in a tree just outside your door.''

''Tell me more.'' Vanessa put aside her pencil and curled up to listen, enthralled.

Realizing her interest was sincere, he settled back to describe his days in the jungle in accurate yet colorful detail. He was finishing his account of his study of pelicans in the Florida Everglades when he stopped speaking and leaned back tiredly against the pillows.

''Afraid I'm beat, Miss Walsh,'' he said. ''Can we continue this interview later?''

''I'm sorry.'' Vanessa arose and went to get a blanket, which she spread solicitously over his feet and legs. ''But don't go to sleep.''

''There's only one thing that can prevent my drifting off,'' he murmured, letting his eyelids droop in a startling manner.

"What? Tell me!" Frightened, Vanessa was instantly crouching beside him.

"The unabridged autobiography of Vanessa Walsh," he teased. "Or," he continued as she leaped to her feet in annoyance, "a brief outline of the highlights."

"You're incorrigible, do you know that?" she retorted, going to put a fresh log on the fire.

"Yes, and you're mysterious. If you tell me about you, I'll tell you about my relationship with Tracey." His gray eyes suddenly sparkled with mischief.

He had hit her squarely in the Achilles' heel of her curiosity, and he knew it. Vanessa paused for a moment, then went slowly back to her chair.

"There's not much to tell," she said, sitting down.

Barret faked a snore.

"Okay, okay!" she cried, shaking him. "I was born in New York, but was brought up by my maternal grandparents

149

on their farm in Maine. My father is Colin Walsh, an international journalist. My mother is Teddi Walsh. She's been a top magazine editor for years. I work for her.'' The admission, unintentionally blurted out, horrified her, and she stopped short, appalled.

''So?'' he said carelessly as he glanced over at her and saw her chagrin. ''I work for my father. And, hey, that growing up on a farm bit explains a lot. Now I know why you're such a great outdoors person.''

''I didn't mean to give you a rundown of my life story,'' she said, looking away in confusion. ''You scared me, and I forgot myself.''

''In your concern for me,'' he said softly. ''Thanks. It's a pleasure finally to know you, Vanessa Walsh.''

''Knowing that I'm working for Mom takes something away from my independent, big-city persona, though, doesn't it?'' She blushed and tried to focus her attention on her notebook.

He shrugged. ''Parents as bosses are usually more demanding than regular employers. They see you as a reflection of themselves; therefore, we're supposed to be all that they aspire to be . . . pretty darn difficult at times. Is that why this story is so important to you? Important enough to risk taking on the wilderness, tree poachers . . . and me?''

''Partly,'' she said. ''But not mostly. You see, I promised my mother I wouldn't do what my predecessor did. Susan Jennings, who previously wrote the column, married the last man she was interviewing to be featured in the magazine. That romance very nearly cost Mom her job. As a result, I promised her adamantly I wouldn't get involved in any kind of emotional relationship with you.''

''I see,'' he said slowly. ''And are you in any danger of breaking your word?'' His gray eyes were penetrating, soul-searching. She couldn't look into them and lie, as she must.

"No," she said, turning to look out the window at the lake and mountains vanishing into the twilight, and struggling desperately to keep any hint of shakiness out of her voice. "But it's not because . . . because I don't care for you. It's because I promised Teddi. Can you understand?" She forced herself to look back at him, desperately hoping he would understand, desperately wanting to say all that was trapped in her heart, pounding to be released.

"Yes," he said softly, and took her cold hand in his. Slowly he raised it, palm open, to his lips, and kissed it. "Yes, blast it, I can."

She shuddered at the warmth of his touch, at the tender way he caressed her skin. She longed to stroke his soft, golden brown hair with trembling fingers, to draw him close, so very close to her.

"Barret, please . . ." she began weakly.

Promise Pending

It had grown dark. The flickering flames in the fireplace provided the only light, and cast bewitching shadows over the gleaming pine walls. Outside, the night was cold and damp, but inside the snug little cabin an intense feeling of warmth and intimacy prevailed. The situation was ripe for romance, and Vanessa knew it. When she felt his fingers tighten about her hand, she could only pray for strength to resist his overwhelming appeal, to have something stop this heady chain of events that were unfolding too fast for her to control.

"Butterfly," he murmured softly, leaning forward to touch his lips to hers. And Vanessa knew she was losing ground fast.

Her prayers, however, were answered in the next heartbeat. The sound of a vehicle careening up the trail stopped them both. Barret leaped to his feet and pulled Vanessa into the deepest of the shadows against the wall near the side door.

"I saw the poachers' faces," he muttered, his own countenance growing tense and hard. ''I can identify them.''

''You think that's them out there, don't you?'' she said, her heart pounding so loudly she feared it might be audible. ''You think they're coming to get you!''

Chapter Ten

"I'm not taking any chances," he said, and picked up the vial of pepper spray from the nearby cupboard.

The vehicle braked to a skidding halt in the rain-slick yard. Vanessa felt her heart thudding heavily as feet bounded across the narrow bit of earth to the cabin and then up the wooden steps to the door beside them.

"Barret! Let me in!"

"Tracey." The word hissed out of Barret's mouth like pent-up steam.

Quickly he drew the dead bolt and let

157

the young woman garbed in camouflage rain gear inside.

Vanessa's heart stopped pounding and sank. She believed she would have preferred the poachers to this beautiful, vibrant woman.

''Get dressed and come with me!'' Tracey ordered without greeting. ''We're to take your canoe across the lake immediately. Aerial surveillance has spotted the poachers at work on trees on the other side.''

''Aerial surveillance?'' Vanessa turned puzzled eyes on Barret.

He paused, then shrugged. ''Vanessa, meet Officer Tracey Coldwell, RCMP. She and I have been working undercover to catch the poachers.''

''Undercover? Are you an RCMP officer too?'' Vanessa asked, astounded.

''No, I simply got roped into the job when I came up here to do research,'' he said ruefully, reaching for a pair of boots and sitting down wearily to put them on.

158

"The RCMP knew I cared about the welfare of the park, and when their security check, like the one your mother ran, revealed I was squeaky-clean of criminal connections and character-weakening vices, they decided I was the perfect cover for Tracey's visits to the park."

"You mean as your girlfriend," Vanessa said, beginning to see the whole picture.

"Right," he said, rising and reaching for a hooded khaki raincoat on a peg by the door. "Okay, Trace, let's get this over with. I take it you've already alerted Jeff and he and some of his rangers are setting up a roadblock on the Pine Point Trail?"

"Of course," she said, shaking back her mane of shining hair. "He was alone at the ranger station at the time, but he assured me he'd get help and be in place and ready when we roust them from this end."

She opened her jacket and reached inside to check a holstered gun.

159

"Do you think you'll need that?" Vanessa asked, startled.

"I'm a law-enforcement officer." She shrugged, pulling her coat shut. "I have to be prepared for resistance. By the way, Barret, what happened to your face? Did Vanessa get fed up and deck you?"

"Very funny," he muttered. "If you must know, I came across our tree-poaching buddies setting a bear trap. The lump is a result of my unsuccessful attempt to apprehend them single-handedly."

"Well, I have a gut feeling they won't be so lucky this time." Tracey set her mouth determinedly. "I'm working on a promotion into a city situation. Catching these guys might just sew it up for me."

"You don't like it here?" Vanessa asked, surprised.

"Here? Mud and bugs and nights so quiet you can hear birds snore? I think not! Now come on, Barry, love. Time's a-wasting."

160

But Barret paused, his gaze on Vanessa.

"Well?" Tracey's voice was insistent.

"Push the canoe off the beach," he said without changing the direction of his stare. "I'll join you in a minute."

Tracey glanced quickly from one to the other, then grinned. "Right. See you in a little while." She opened the door but paused before stepping out into the swirling fog. "A little while, Barry, no longer."

"Vanessa, I'm sorry, really sorry I got you involved in all this," he said once Tracey had gone. "When I first learned about your coming I pictured a tough investigative journalist and figured our brand of criminal would be small stuff to that kind of big-city girl. But you aren't. And these guys are proving they can be violent. As soon as I get back, regardless of the outcome, I'm shipping you off to New York. This whole situation is a mess."

"A mess?"

"Yes, a certifiable mess. Beyond the poacher problem, you promised your mother you wouldn't get involved and now . . ."

"And now what?" She managed to keep her voice calm in spite of the fact that every ounce of her body was taut, every facet of her soul trembling.

"Haven't you noticed?" He looked so deeply into Vanessa's eyes, she feared he might be reading her mind. "I'm definitely entering the danger zone."

"No . . . no," Vanessa stammered. "I thought . . . I mean . . . I . . ."

"You thought it was Tracey and me," he said, gently putting strong hands on her shoulders. "You thought you and I were becoming good friends, nothing more. And that's one of the reasons you're totally irresistible . . . you're completely unassuming, totally guileless, a sincerely honest person with integrity to burn. You're as genuine as this beautiful

162

park, as capable of being at home here as I am.

"But you made a promise to your mother . . . a promise that you feel you must fulfill. You will never be happy unless you do. I understand and respect your decision."

"Barret . . ." Vanessa raised a hand weakly in protest, but he silenced her.

"I'd appreciate it if you got packing. I'll take you to the airport first thing in the morning. Your leaving immediately is the only solution."

Chapter Eleven

Obediently, hopelessly, Vanessa packed her bags, then curled up on the couch near the fire to wait for the outcome of his night's adventures. At first she hadn't worried. After all, he was with a trained police officer, and there was aerial surveillance and Jeff and his rangers as backup, wasn't there, she thought.

But when midnight came and passed and he hadn't returned, she began to feel uneasy. She made a pot of coffee and drank a scalding cup black. She paced the hardwood floors. Finally, in desperation, she had scrubbed her tiny bathroom. Then, just before dawn, she fell asleep in a chair by the living room window.

When she awoke, the first light of a new day was struggling in between a small crack in the draperies. She arose, stretched, opened the curtains, turned toward the kitchen—and gasped.

Barret sat at the kitchen table dirtier than she had ever seen him. His battered Snowy River hat lay on the countertop, drenched and muddy. He looked as though he were soaked to the skin, but he was making no move to change. His face was ashen.

"Are you all right?" she asked, going quickly to him.

"No," he said tiredly. "It's impossible to be okay when you've just been responsible for putting a friend in jail."

"What friend?" Aghast, Vanessa sank into a chair opposite him. "Surely not Tracey?"

"Tracey?" He scoffed with derision.

168

"Definitely not. Actually, as a result of our work tonight, I believe she's well on her way to that big-city promotion she wants so desperately. She couldn't care less about the park or any of us who live here. All that counted for her was getting ahead in her profession."

"Well, then, who are you talking about?" Vanessa was growing exasperated in her nervousness.

"Jeff," he said shortly. He ran a hand agitatedly through his hair and avoided her eyes. "Jeff was in league with the poachers. He was keeping his rangers away from areas where they were at work. The reason he got me tangled up in your magazine story wasn't just as a prank, either. He suspected me of helping the RCMP and figured that if he got a reporter up here to interview me I'd be kept too busy to bother his colleagues in crime. He knew I was getting close to the truth; I was one of the few people who knew of his addiction."

169

"Addiction? To what?" Vanessa was shocked. "Drugs, alcohol?"

"Video gambling," he said tiredly, as if the words took the last of his strength. "That's how he got into this mess in the first place. He'd borrowed money to finance his habit from men who turned out to be tree poachers. They deliberately allowed him to become heavily indebted to them. Then, when he couldn't pay them back, they forced him to help in their criminal activities.

"When I learned how deeply in debt he was, I started giving him money to help him out of the mess. Every time he took my financial help, he vowed he would get help in beating his habit. And every time he failed to do it.

"I was upset, but I never once suspected how desperate he was; desperate enough to risk his reputation and career. I failed him miserably. And now he's in handcuffs along with the actual poachers,

170

his career ruined, probably on his way to a jail sentence.''

''You can't blame yourself,'' she said gently. She placed her hand on his arm. ''You did what you could, what you thought was best.''

''Right.'' Barret ignored her attempt to soothe him and stood up abruptly. ''Are you packed? I'll take you to the airport now.''

''You should get some rest,'' she said. ''I can catch a plane tomorrow.''

''No!'' he snapped, grabbing his wet hat and slapping it onto his head. ''You'll go now! I don't need to be responsible for costing anyone else their job today! I'll get your bags and wait in the Jeep.''

The drive from the cabin to the airport was as silent as the drive from the airport to the cabin had been. Fog again had closed in over the mountain roads to make the journey treacherous.

At the airport Barret did not wait to see her off. He had a lot of work to do before

171

the snow came, he said. He shook her hand, wished her farewell, and vanished into the same kind of swirling mist out of which he had appeared less than a week earlier.

Chapter Twelve

Vanessa sat curled up on the window seat in her bedroom in the farmhouse in Maine. It was Christmas Eve, and it had begun to snow again; big, benign-looking flakes drifting softly down to join those on the already snow-covered ground.

Across a wide expanse of lawn in front of the large red barn, her grandparents were unhitching a fine team of Percherons from a big green sleigh. Her five-foot-six-inch, hundred-and-forty-pound grandmother was every bit as adept at handling the huge horses as was her six-foot-three-inch, barrel-chested grandfather. Hers had definitely never been a family of passive, spiritless women, she thought. Until now. Until she had walked unprotestingly away from the best thing she had ever known.

She arose and went to her small, schoolgirl desk near the bed. For another, countless time she picked up the postcard made from a photo of Buster sitting on his haunches by the lake, the butterfly perched saucily on his head, and read its few words: *Merry Christmas from Mac, Tosh, Buster, and Barret.*

Was that all there was to be? she cried inwardly. Was that all he had to say after all they had shared. . . . ? If it was, then probably it was just as well she had left him to his hermit's existence.

"Vannie, will you come down here for a minute?" Her mother's voice brought her out of her unhappy thoughts.

"Sure." She welcomed the distraction and hurried downstairs, comfortable in jeans and a soft blue cotton sweater after two months of playing dress-up in the publishing house in New York.

Her cheeks were still bright from the recent family sleigh ride as she entered the big, old-fashioned parlor where a log fire crackled on the hearth and a huge balsam fir Christmas tree dominated the bay window. Her parents were on the couch, her mother looking incredibly young and unsophisticated in jeans and a pink cashmere sweater, her father overpoweringly handsome, as always, as he sat with his arm draped casually but possessively over his wife's shoulders.

''Are you enjoying the job?'' he asked without preamble. Vanessa suppressed a smile.

''Cut right to the chase, eh, Dad?'' She grinned. ''You'll never change.''

''That's the journalist in me.'' He smiled back. ''Hang the preliminaries. That's why I proposed to your mother the first time we met. Now don't try to change the subject, Ms. Walsh. We want

177

the truth, the whole truth, and nothing—''

"Okay, okay!" Vanessa held up a silencing hand, paused, and looked helplessly at her mother. "Teddi . . . Mom . . ."

"It's okay, honey," her mother surprised her by replying kindly. "I'll understand. I've read your article and . . ." Suddenly Teddi Walsh, the consummate professional and famously articulate journalist, was at a loss for words.

"And you can see I'm not meant to be a writer," Vanessa finished for her.

"Baby, I'm sorry." Teddi arose and went to put a manicured hand on her daughter's arm.

"Well, I'm not!" Vanessa glanced excitedly from her mother to her father. "I never wanted to be a magazine writer. I was doing it only to please both of you."

"Really?" Teddi was visibly relieved. "What do you want to do? Tell us. We'll help."

178

"I want to be a biologist," she said. "I want to go back to school, get my degree, and then work in environmental conservation."

"Really?" Colin Walsh's surprise was so obviously feigned that Vanessa turned quickly toward him, just in time to catch him winking at her mother. "Why did you decide on that branch of study?"

"Well . . ." Vanessa proceeded slowly, her suspicions starting to rise. "I loved the outdoors when I was growing up here on the farm, and I never stopped being curious about every living thing and admiring it. In high school my best marks were in science, biology in particular. I would have pursued that line of study except—"

"Except, being a dutiful daughter, you tried to please us." Colin arose and joined his wife and daughter, putting an arm around each. "Well, you gave it your best shot. Better than your best shot, I'd say,

179

considering all you gave up toward that end.''

''All I gave up . . . ?'' Vanessa faced her parents, confused.

In reply Colin went to the kitchen door, opened it, and said, ''You can come in now. We've paved the way.''

A tall, broad-shouldered figure appeared in the doorway. For a moment Vanessa couldn't believe the man in a sheepskin-collared rancher's coat and tan pants was who she knew it to be. A new Snowy River hat was in his right hand.

''Hello, Vanessa.'' The voice rocked her memory and made her light-headed with joy.

''Barret, what are you doing here?'' she asked, trying to disguise the extent of her pleasure.

''I've come to recruit a research assistant,'' he said seriously, although his eyes were twinkling. ''I need someone who has a professional knowledge of expository writing to assist me in preparing documentation to present to an upcoming government commission on the fate of Mount Kingsland Park. I thought you might be able to recommend someone. And I had to return this.'' He pulled his left hand, which he had been hiding behind his back, into view. In it he held her battered tilly hat. ''I know what store you placed on it, even facing down a four-hundred-pound bear on one occasion to retrieve it. I figured the least I could do was see it safely returned one more time.''

Totally confused, Vanessa looked at her parents. They were remaining as blank and uninvolved as possible, yet she could see a conspiracy was under way.

''What's going on here?'' she asked slowly but with a racing pulse.

''Honey,'' Teddi said, coming to take her daughter by the arm. ''I am a woman who has been in love with one man for . . . many years . . . and I recognize the symptoms. I can also appreciate the effort

181

it must have taken for you to walk away from him just because you believed you were doing what your mother needed you to do.''

''We love you, baby, but this guy tells us he does too,'' Colin said, grinning and going to slap Barret companionably on the back. ''And it's time you had someone of your own. If you want him, of course. I understand it would mean living in that cabin of his for long periods of time, out in the country every day, chasing birds, bees, etc. I'm not telling you what to do, you understand, but if I were you, I'd give Barret's plans some serious thought.''

''I think your father just proposed for me.'' Barret was grinning too. ''All that's left for me to do is wait for the answer.''

''Barret . . .'' Vanessa felt as if she had been hit by a tornado, a big, powerful, love-filled tornado.

''Say 'Yes, Barret,' '' he prompted gently, and suddenly she was in his arms.

"Yes, Barret," she whispered, fighting back tears of happiness. "But why did you take so long to come? Didn't you know how I felt?"

"You were bound by that promise," he said. "After what I did to Jeff, I wasn't about to risk harming anyone else's career. Furthermore, I wanted to give you a chance to see if writing was what you really wanted to do with your life. I didn't want you to regret any decision you made later regarding you and me."

"Barret called me the day after you returned," Teddi astonished her daughter by explaining, as she stood sheltered in the arm of her husband. "He told me point-blank how he felt about you, but said he didn't want to stand in the way of any career choices Colin and I had made for you, and which you yourself genuinely wanted to pursue. So I told him I'd turn a cold, strictly objective eye on your writing ability and your state of happiness

183

in the publishing business and let him know my conclusions.''

''And as a result you realized I wasn't destined to be the next Virginia Woolf and was forcing myself along at work?'' Vanessa snuggled close to Barret's tall, muscular body and could barely speak, she was so happy.

''I watched you carefully,'' Teddie continued. ''And reread your story on Barret time and time again. And discovered that while it lacked style, technique, and sparkle, it did have an underlying sense of passion for that park . . . and one special person.

''I knew then what had to be done. I called Colin and told him he had to come home at once. Then I contacted Barret. They both arrived shortly after noon today. Barret hid in the barn while we took you on that sleigh ride to give him an opportunity to sneak into the house and surprise you.''

''It also gave your mother time to size

184

him up.'' Colin chuckled, brushing a kiss over his wife's sleek golden hair. ''Her protective maternal instincts had to be satisfied before she could give her blessing . . . believe it or not!''

''Colin, I'm sure there's a flight back to that unpronounceable country from which you came sometime this evening.'' Teddi was flushing. ''Just keep it up and see how fast I can book you aboard.''

''Oh, no, you won't, not before tonight, my darling,'' he muttered, pulling her close. ''Definitely not before tonight.'' His lips brushed his wife's temple in a sensuous, suggestive manner. Then he turned to Barret.

''Why you don't take our daughter for a walk in this beautiful Christmas Eve snowfall, young man?'' He winked at Barret. ''Her mother and I would like to be alone.''

''Certainly, sir.'' Barret continued the game of exaggerated Victorian manners. ''And if we're gone a length of time you find improper, I will most definitely marry her; you have my word.''

''A true gentleman.'' Colin bowed from the waist. ''Take her away, young sir. Take her away.''

Barret threw an arm about Vanessa's shoulders and guided her into the entrance hall, where the coats hung. But before she could stoop to pull on her snow boots, he caught her into his arms and kissed her soundly, holding her so tightly she felt the breath being squeezed out of her body.

''I love you, Butterfly,'' he muttered. ''Love you, love you, love you.''

Vanessa had never felt happier. Freed from the cocoon of a pending promise, she was about to spread her wings and fly. She knew the flight would be magical.